Tomorrow's Journal

Tomorrow's Journal

Dominick Cancilla

Cemetery Dance Publications
Baltimore
2019

Cemetery Dance Publications
132B Industry Lane, Unit #7
Forest Hill, MD 21050
www.cemeterydance.com

Trade Paperback Edition

ISBN: 978-1-58767-665-9

Cover Artwork © 2019 by Desert Isle Design, LLC
Interior Design © 2019 by Desert Isle Design, LLC

DO NOT REMOVE THE BINDER CLIPS.

The clips are there to hold the pages closed until the proper time. This sounds like a ridiculous instruction, but you need to take it very, very seriously:

DO NOT LOOK AHEAD IN THIS JOURNAL.

DO NOT TURN SO MUCH AS THE CORNER OF A SINGLE PAGE WITHOUT FIRST READING THESE INSTRUCTIONS THOROUGHLY.

This journal is like absolutely nothing you have ever had before. It looks old because it IS old. It looks valuable because it IS valuable. It's not just something to write in, it's an opportunity. You only get one shot at this, and if you don't do EXACTLY as I say, you are going to have to live with the pain of failure for the rest of your life.

You and I are going to write to each other through this journal. You will write a message; I will write back; you will respond.

We are going to start with a little exercise to get you used to this. Get a pen and write something—just a single short sentence—at the bottom of this page. Write anything you want. After you have written, AND ONLY THEN, remove the binder clips and carefully turn a SINGLE page.

Mom — your kidding, right?

DO NOT TURN THE PAGE AGAIN UNTIL INSTRUCTED.

This journal has nothing to do with your mother. Mom didn't put it under your pillow. She doesn't know about it, and you can never tell her, your dad, or anyone else about it. Also, as someone who aspires to be a writer, you should know better when to use a contraction and when to use a possessive. It's embarrassing.

That should be enough to convince you that I can read what you write. This situation is as delicate as it is unbelievable, and if you want the miracle to continue, you must remember these ~~eight~~ basic rules:

1. NEVER look ahead, read ahead, or so much as glance at a page before it's time. If you drop the journal, turn your head and pick it up so you don't accidentally see something you shouldn't.

2. Whenever you are done with the journal, replace the binder clips so that any pages you haven't already seen are held closed.

3. When you write, use as many pages as you need to. It's okay to turn a page if you need more room. If you need to stop writing and start again later, draw a line across the page.

4. Only after you are COMPLETELY sure you have finished writing your message to me can you turn the page to see my response. My responses will always start on the next left-hand page after the one on which you finished writing. If you finish writing on a left-hand page, leave the right-hand page blank and turn the page to see my response.

5. After you have turned a page to see my response, you may no longer make changes or additions to what you wrote.

6. ~~If you turn the page and there is no response, replace the binder clips, put the book aside, and wait for instructions. It may be a very long wait, so be patient.~~

7. If my response takes more than one page, it's okay to turn the page to continue reading.

8. It's okay to reread past entries in our conversation, but only AFTER you have replaced the binder clips to avoid an accident.

Read that list again and memorize it.

I have knowledge and experience that you cannot imagine I have. This allows me to know many of the consequences of your actions even before you take them. Because I have this knowledge, I have an additional list of instructions that you must obey. Some of these are going to sound weird and arbitrary, but every single one of them is of utmost importance.

Dos and Don'ts List:

- Do follow all of my instructions to the letter, no matter how ridiculous they may sound.

- Don't have anything to do with guns. Don't even let yourself be in the same room as one.

- Don't take the journal out of your room.

- Don't call 911 if you hurt your head in the house.

- Don't put this journal on your desk when your wallet is on the desk.

- Do put your laundry away before Mom has to ask.

- Don't post to Facebook about what you'd do with a million dollars.

- Don't take the bus ~~to come home from getting the brush.~~ ever.

-

-

I know that's a lot to process. Read it all over again, think hard about it, and then write any questions you have on the facing page.

I'm pretty solidly weirded out by this right now. It really did seem like you responded to what I wrote, but that's impossible since what you wrote is already printed in the book. If it was a lucky guess by whoever published this thing, then it was the most amazing guess ever. Maybe someone who knows me really well printed this and guessed that I'd assume Mom left it for me to find so she could pretend it was some kind of magic item. It wouldn't be the first time she tried to trick me into thinking that magic wasn't bullshit.

The only other even barely reasonable thing I can think of is that the book has a computer built into the back cover, it's using handwriting analysis to read what I write and e-ink or something to write the responses, and the responses are coming from either the computer or someone on wifi. You don't want me to look ahead because you don't want me to see the computer or notice that the later pages are glued together to hide a hollow with a computer in it. That would be pretty complicated, though, and if the technology existed I bet I'd have read about it online by now.

That leaves miracles, angels, demons, space aliens, and other crap too ridiculous to consider.

I guess it could be that you are psychic and are using telepathy to read my mind when I write and telekinesis or something to put the words on the paper before

I turn the page. I don't believe in any of that stuff, either. You might as well just say Jesus is writing it and leave it at that. There's no real evidence and this book isn't evidence until there's no other possible explanation.

To be thorough, I suppose I should consider that I might be insane and writing to myself, but I'm not, and even if I was, I don't know how I'd do the parts that look pre-printed. Maybe someone knocked me out after I wrote the sentence and then woke me up after they'd printed a response but come on, really? I'd just as soon go with the psychic one as that.

It's got to be something else. I'm going to figure this out. I just need more time. If that first answer wasn't a fluke and you can give me good answers to what I'm writing now, it's a headscrambling magic trick no matter how you're doing it.

You asked for questions, so here are mine:

- Why can't I do the things on the list? The laundry one is so random it makes me think maybe you really are Mom.

- Why are some things crossed out?

- Why are there empty bullets? Did you forget to write something? Is it a computer malfunction?

- Since you're not my parents, can I assume that I'm not supposed to be watching my language here? I'd like the option of telling you to fuck off if this turns out to be a pranking jerk move of some kind.

You aren't going to figure out how this works on your own, but I will tell you in more detail a little later. I'm also going to be introducing you to someone who will open your eyes about not only this book, but also a great many things. You have to be patient.

Answering your questions:

You can't do the things on the list because if you do, the project that we are going to work on together will be ruined. I know that your doing any of these will have a bad outcome, but—for some very complicated reasons—in most cases I have no idea what that outcome would be. For example, I don't know why your not putting your laundry away would ruin things, but I do know that it would. Maybe if you don't put it away Mom sees it in your room, goes in to do something about it, sees the journal, and messes things up by reading it. I don't know for sure. That's just a possibility.

There may be times when I have to cross things out after I have written them. For example, it might be that an instruction was too specific and had to be made broader to avoid a wider range of problems. Because of the way this journal works, I can go back and make additions to what I have written if there's empty space, or cross things out if writing them was a mistake or they need to be changed or clarified. That won't work for you so don't try it.

That also explains why there are empty bullets in the bulleted list and empty space after the numbered list. When I wrote the Do/Don't list I had only four items for it, but I made 10 bullets so I could go back later and add instructions as they came up or as I remembered things I should have included.

Foul language doesn't offend me, but you should avoid it because it's a sign you're getting worked up about something. You need to remain calm for all this to work out.

Any more questions before we continue?

I'll tell you why I think rule #6 was crossed out later when I explain more about how the journal works. It's very complicated and I don't want to go into it yet.

Who are you?

What should I call you?

If you are writing the responses, why are they printed on the paper instead of handwritten?

If you aren't one of my parents, how did you get the book into my room?

How can you not know why you did things?

Why can't I read ahead?

I don't want to tell you who I am just yet because it's complicated. If you play by the rules, everything should go smoothly and I think I end up telling you who I am next Monday.

Don't call me anything. It's just the two of us having this conversation, so we don't need to use any names beyond pronouns. Also, it would feel weird to me if you called me by name. You'll understand that better soon, but for now I'll just promise that I'm not some creepy stalker or something.

I can't handwrite because I'm disabled. I have a condition that makes fine motor movements difficult. I'm using something, a technology I'll say, that can print on any surface the way a printer can print on paper. It's mentally controlled so I don't have to use my hands too much. The only drawback is that it can't erase, so I have to be careful.

Don't forget that even though I'm using print, this isn't a pre-printed book in the normal sense. My responses have been in the book since you first received it, but DO NOT be tempted to look ahead and see what they are. I wrote my words in response to what you wrote, so if you read what I write before you write what I responded to it could change what you write which would change what I write and what you saw. That's obviously impossible so don't do it. I don't know what would happen if you did, but it couldn't be good. Most likely, my writing would stop being correct responses to yours and this whole thing would fall apart. Trust me, we don't want that to happen.

I don't know why I wrote some things in the book because I have no memory of why I wrote them. Either my writing those things changed your behavior so that my reason for writing it disappeared, or it's something I added later that you're seeing as you read but I don't see because I haven't written it yet. This may sound like a literal word salad, but it will make more sense after you know how the journal works. For now, it's more important that we concentrate on other things.

Sorry, I skipped one of your questions. I didn't put the book in your room and I honestly don't know how it got there. Someone else did it. How that is possible will become somewhat more clear later. I can't go into it now because it wouldn't make any sense and would take too long to explain.

Anything else? I know you have at least one more question.

Where are you?

I'm in the same room you are, but a long time from when you are reading this.

The next thing you want to write is "Prove it."

It's not possible for me to prove where I am. I could tell you anything you like about your house or your room, but all that would prove would be that I've been there, not that I'm there now. What I can do is prove that I know you very well.

When you got Dad's old car for your sweet 16 you were secretly disappointed you didn't get a new one, then felt guilty when you overheard your parents trying to figure out how they were going to afford the increase in car insurance.

You're secretly saving up for a trip to New York after you graduate and have been squirreling away cash in an envelope taped under your desk drawer, but even though you have more than a year left to save you'll never have enough if you keep treating it as mad money instead of as savings.

The instep of your left foot itches. It's athlete's foot from the gym at school. You need to get some spray to take care of that.

I know it wouldn't be impossible for someone to figure these things out, but they should be good enough for now. Any reasonable person would be convinced, so maybe you will be, too.

Crap! I started the trip fund with babysitting money, and that reminds me that I was supposed to leave for the Atkinsons in five minutes and I'm not even dressed.

The rules say not to take the journal so I'll leave it, even though it's kind of insulting that you don't trust me enough to take care of it. Can we talk more after I get back?

(Also, effu for the "reasonable person" crack.)

DON'T GO. Cancel the babysitting. Say you're sick or something. You'll be happy you did.

Trust me.

I think I'd regret losing the money more than I'd regret not being able waste an evening writing in my new magic journal. Talk to you tonight!

(Drawing line as per rules) ->

Well that was fucked up.

The Atkinsons' baby is named Emilia, and she usually just goes to bed and sleeps while I earn money for sitting around doing my homework, reading, or catching up on Facebook, but tonight she started bawling the second her parents left and just would not shut up. I wanted to give her a bottle, but they won't let me use a microwave to heat one and their bottle-warmer thing was broken, so I had to heat water on the stove like I'm living in the woods. I needed to hold Emilia because when I didn't she freaked, so I was trying to do the bottle one-handed when she completely flipped out and started thrashing around. It totally caught me by surprise, and somehow or other she managed to thwack the water pot. I grabbed it—to make sure it didn't fall and instead knocked it off the stove and onto my leg.

I had let the water heat too long so it was almost boiling, which is too hot for a bottle, but I was having trouble paying attention because Emilia was literally going insane. That's why the water was so hot that

I got a burn on my leg and Emilia got an even worse burn on her hand. I tried to put ice on both of us, but you can imagine that she was completely freaking out at that point. I ended up putting her in the bath so I could at least keep cool water on her burn.

By the time the Atknsons got home I had everything cleaned up, but Emilia was still awake and the burn on her hand looked nasty. They were seething unhappiness in that kind of quiet, stern way that is scarier than being yelled at. Thank whatever I could walk home because driving with one of them would have been coated-in-lead uncomfortable.

I'll be surprised if they ever call me for babysitting again. They didn't even mention paying me.

I really hope Emilia is okay. I feel more stressed out about her being hurt than I do about them being mad at me or not being paid. She's usually a good baby and I still love her even though she had a bad night. I wouldn't ever want anything bad to happen to her. I feel really guilty for letting her get hurt when I was in charge.

When I got home Dad was kind of in his own little world again, looking through one of his old design books, but Mom definitely noticed something was wrong. I told her I just had a bad evening and went to my room, but downplaying it like that felt like lying.

You were incredibly right when you told me I shouldn't have gone babysitting. I am so sorry. I promise to listen to you from here on.

You're sorry now and you're going to be even more sorry later, but that's too far in the future to be as strong a lesson as it should be. There's nothing you can do about it now and nothing you can do about the nightmares you're going to have when you finally fall asleep.

The best thing you can do is keep reminding yourself that this journal isn't a game to play or a puzzle for you to figure out. I really do have answers that you don't even know the questions to yet. You are in the past to me, so I can remember things you haven't done. That doesn't mean I know everything, but it does mean that I can see a big picture that in your view is only starting to be painted.

I'm glad you promised to listen. Let's let Emilia be the only lesson you need to start taking me more seriously?

I think I'd have to take this seriously if you really are from the future.

You're asking me to believe that this book is a kind of time travel, then? It would have to be some amazing technology if it can send text to the future as I write it and then send your words to the past for me to read. But if you can send a book back in time, why couldn't you send back videos or computers or something to make this easier for me? Maybe you can send something that will prove you're from the future, like money with a future date on it. Can you send me something like that?

This isn't time travel, it's magic. Don't let that fact start you thinking about Mom again, though. She isn't like your grandmother was. Your mom says she does magic, but she couldn't light a candle without a pile of ingredients, an hour of chanting, and a book of matches. The ceremonies at her Coven are like a child in a play-kitchen going through the motions of making dinner. They're an excuse that has more to do with making them feel the way any religion makes its true believers feel than with drawing in energy from the universe. They accomplish nothing substantial.

This book is powerful stuff; literally world-changing stuff. It's magic more complicated and intricate than you can even imagine. It's the kind of thing your grandmother did.

Got that?

I assume you mean Mom's mom. I never met her, but Mom talks about her as if she could divine what was going to be in the mail each day and the only thing keeping her from flying was her lack of an appropriate broom. It makes for good stories, but I highly doubt any of it was real so she's not a great example if you're trying to impress me.

That said, since you can make magic books, are you a good witch or a bad witch?

There is no real witchcraft as your family understands it, no religious ceremonies that have actual power, and no mystical rites that can get anything done in and of themselves. There is real magic. I can't do any of it but I'm trying to learn and am working with someone who can. I'm not sure how she got this journal and I have just as little idea of how it was created as you do. It's just a tool that was given to me the same way it was given to you. I'm using it to get you to help me because it's too late for me to do what needs to be done and there is no other way I can contact you.

There are things I need you to do if you are going to help me. Lots of things. The sooner we get past these questions and on to the real work the better.

It's funny you say that there's no real witchcraft when you already literally said that my grandmother could do it three pages ago. Mom definitely believes. Did you know that when I was little she once got furious because she came home and Dad was letting me watch "The Wizard of Oz"? She thought it was ridiculous with the way it showed witches. Dad calmed her down, we all finished the movie and had a nice talk about what "real" witches were like. Mom was cool with the Wizard of Oz after that, but pretty much never let me see anything else with witches, fairy godmothers, or any of the rest of that kind of thing in it. I've never seen a Disney cartoon. I'm probably the most Disdeprived person in a hundred-mile radius.

It's weird that you'd send me a paper journal; I wouldn't think they'd still use paper in the future. Why not make a magic iPad or something and send that back instead of a book? Writing is slow and tedious. It makes me feel like Granny McFeeble.

Let's say for the moment that I buy your future story. Is it all flying cars, jet packs, and weird slang words where you come from? Can you plug stuff into your brain instead of going to school or reading books? You said you're in this house, but is it all computerized rooms and robot butlers now?

Tell me all about the future!

This journal is the only thing of its kind and even though you're the first in your immediate family to have it, it's been in your family for decades. I can't say more than that.

Regarding the future, I could tell you more but I probably shouldn't. I don't know how that might affect things and I want there to be as few variables as possible. It's hard enough messing with the past without complicating it by giving you knowledge of too many things that haven't happened yet.

I will tell you that we do still use paper. We probably use it more than you do, actually. The big picture is more "Planet of the Apes" than it is "Star Trek," though. That's why I need your help.

I'd like to move on now.

No way you're leaving it there — this is too big an opportunity!

Can you tell me small things about the future, like things that are going to happen to me? Can you give me the answers to tests before I take them so I can get my grades up?

How about, if I tell you something I want to do, can you tell me how it will work out so I won't waste my time doing things that aren't going to work? I still have a couple of years before I have to worry about college, but I was thinking of majoring in English composition or some kind of literature, because I read a lot and I'm going to be doing a lot of writing. Would one of those be the right decision?

If that's too broad, what should I do about the essay we're supposed to write in Mr. Parkers'? We were assigned to do a "what does it mean to me" glurgepiece on the "Road not Taken" poem because P says the poem is about how not following the crowd can lead you to a better life. I raised my hand and said that maybe taking that other path ruined his life, so he should have done what everyone else did.

Before he could even answer, Olivia raised her hand — which is practically a once-in-a-lifetime experience. Important aside: Am I supposed to tell you who people are or assume that you already know? Olivia is this gothemo girl that's in the same grade as me. We have a couple of classes together. She always wears black jeans and black T-shirts with the names of bands normal people don't listen to. I don't think I've ever seen her talk to anyone except for teachers who ask her questions, and even then she talks like the words are being dragged out of a tar pit.

Anyway, P calls on her because it's the first time she's spoken in class of her own free will, and she says she agrees that it's probably a poem warning you away from the popular. She starts to go on about how the poem is in "yellow woods" and Lovecraft used yellow to (something-about-monsters). It was weird how much she was into this.

P was kind of stunned, I guess. He said that the poem is definitely about the benefits of not conforming, but if we wanted to try and make an argument for something else, we could. I don't know about what Olivia was talking about, but I think my original nonfreaky point was right. Here's my question: Should I write the essay about a life being ruined by the other path, or should I stick with what P wants because it's safer? I'd rather do my own thing, but I don't want to get a bad grade because he's biased against originality.

Did you know I'm also working on a novel? It's called

"Maid With Love" and it's about a maid in Jane Austen-time England who is secretly in love with the adult son of the master of her house. She has these detailed fantasies where she's the secret daughter of Queen Victoria and sweeps her paramour off his feet, but she has to learn to be brave in real life and not just in her dreams. I'm going to start outlining it after reading all of Jane Austen's books for research, which I'm going to do starting this semester or maybe in the summer. Can you tell me how the manuscript sells and what I had to do to sell it? And if they ever make it into a movie? Would it do better if the boyfriend is a vampire? Or is that way too much to reveal?

I also have this other idea for a novel about a woman with an awful husband that she has to get rid of but can't bring herself to. I've got the first sentence all ready: "She loved her husband the way you love a familiar old sweater that you wish you could get rid of because it chafes and occasionally beats you." Isn't that the best? I haven't got much past that, except that I want to have a scene where it's like fencing but with big kitchen knives, although I'm not sure if I want that in this book or the "olde England" one. Which one do you think I should write first?

I write short stories, too. My Facebook friends all think my stories are great. I think I'm going to make a collection and sell it on Amazon. There's a lot of things I could use the money for.

Can you give me relationship info, too? Like, can you tell me what I need to do to get Colin to ask me out? He's in algebra with me and has eyes so blue I could drown in them but that I hardly ever see because he barely looks at me. He's on the swim team and the other day they were practicing before class started and I almost walked into a pole because I was trying to watch while I was walking. Do you already know about him? If I wanted to give him some kind of secret-admirer present, do you have a suggestion?

Yes, I know who Colin was and that you like writing and reading. I don't mind you giving me little details of your life in case I've forgotten them, but remember that I probably already know anything like that you'd think to tell me. I'd tell you that I'd appreciate your being concise unless we're discussing something directly involved with our plans but I know that would be futile.

I can't help you with tests, both because it's pointless in the big picture and because there's no way I can remember or look up what the test questions were back in your time. I'll have to ask you not to look for help with short-term problems like that unless they are truly urgent. Writing this journal is difficult for me and I don't want to waste my time playing what amounts to games.

In a certain sense, I can tell you whether something you want to do will work out or not. That's going to be a big part of what we're doing, and it's why I set out rules for things you must and cannot do.

If it helps, I can at least tell you that aside from a surprise quiz tomorrow in history you will never have to take another test if you follow my instructions. You're not going to college. Don't ask why because I won't tell you. You also will never write either of those novels if you don't go along with the plans that I will be giving you, so don't bother asking any more about them.

One thing I would suggest is that you write down any story ideas you have that you haven't yet gotten down. You wouldn't want to forget them and you may not have the opportunity to do any significant creative writing for a while.

I can tell you about Colin and in fact I intended to do so even if you didn't bring him up.

Don't go out with Colin. Forget about him. I don't think he'll ever ask you out, but if he does, turn him down. You aren't going to take my word on this even after what happened with Emilia, so I'll tell you that if you do go out with him he ends up assaulting you in a way I'm not even going to describe and it traumatizes you for the rest of your life.

Story ideas:

- Weight: A girl who can gain or lose weight anywhere on her body she wants overnight

- Jasmine's Collection: A girl who can make friends with insects

- Picture This: A girl who the whole town thinks will never amount to much but turns out to be a famous artist

- Bat Weather: This girl goes to bed but then wakes up the next morning with vampire powers, except she's a vegetarian and can go in the sun

- Flame Queen: A girl who is always shunned because she isn't popular, but one day finds that she can throw flame from her hands and goes on a rampage burning down cheerleaders and etc.

- Hunger artist: Girl who is the REAL hero in the Hunger Games universe because she's the one who actually taught Katniss to use a bow, but told her to say it was her father so nobody would know the secret

Also need to make a list of all the words I've created to help me get in the OED when I'm famous.

I'm calling bullshit, Emilia or not. Colin isn't like that at all. You're right that I don't trust you enough to take your word that he's a violent rapist/whatever.

Here's why it doesn't make sense. If you know that Colin is going to assault me, that means that at some point I end up going out with Colin, he assaults me, and you find out about it. But if you're trying to convince me not to go out with him, that means that you think you can help me avoid getting assaulted. But if what you say lets me avoid being assaulted, then you in the future wouldn't know he'd assault me and wouldn't know to warn me. That means that either I'm not going to listen to you about Colin no matter what you say or in the future he didn't actually assault me so you can't be sure he would have.

What do you say to that, smart guy?

What I say is that you're a pain in the ass.

Here's the deal: You're right that from my perspective Colin never assaulted you because what I've written in this journal convinces you to never go out with him. Technically, I suppose that also means that I don't know that he would assault you if you went out with him.

However, what I DO know is that if I write "don't or he's going to assault you," then you keep writing in this journal. I can infer from that that if I don't stop you from going out with Colin, you won't continue writing. So even though I don't know exactly what would happen if you went out with Colin, I know that if I don't stop you from going out with him something happens that stops you from writing in this journal. Maybe he assaults you and traumatizes you, maybe the two of you get in a car accident, maybe he breaks your heart and you just give up on doing anything productive until it's too late, maybe something else—I don't know the details.

You're going to ask how I know you'll stop writing if I don't warn you away from Colin. When I write certain things, there's a sensation like a shift toward calm. I can't describe it exactly, but it's a feeling that something has changed for the better, like when you suddenly wake up to the realization that the horrible thing happening to you was just a dream.

I know that when I wrote that Colin would assault you, something changed. That means that there was a reality in which something happened to stop you from writing, and I had to write something in the journal to change your behavior. I don't know what that behavior was because from my perspective it never happened, but I do know that I had to write what I wrote.

You're going to reread those last two paragraphs and decide it's a load of crap-trash, but I promise you couldn't explain it any better even if you understood it completely, and you never will.

Also, I didn't mean for you to write your story ideas in here. Put them somewhere more permanent instead.

Monkey-flinging ass-grabbed craptrash is right. You can't even tell me what will happen if I make different choices? What good are you if you don't know what would have happened instead? How can I trust you if you don't even know whether or not what you're telling me is true? Sounds less like psychic, more like mental problems to me.

Calm down.

I know your future, but I don't know all possible futures. You can't think back to last year and know how summer would have gone differently if you hadn't been playing with one of Mom's candles and accidentally set her spirit altar on fire. I can't remember the effects of actions you didn't take because they didn't happen.

I'm far from useless, though. Because I know your future, I can write instructions in this journal that try and stop you from screwing things up for us. I can also tell you things to do that will lead to good outcomes.

I'll give you one of those now. There's a boy in algebra who sits second from the back in the corner by the window. You've noticed him because he dresses really well, doesn't talk much, and has black hair. I think he's Hispanic. His name is Patrick. At lunch, when you're going back to your ~~locket~~ locker, you're going to see him arguing with some guys. I want you to walk up to him, ignoring the other guys and looking like you know Patrick really well. Put a hand gently on his shoulder and say, in a normal speaking voice so that everyone can hear, "I can't stop thinking about last night. Don't forget to text me when you get home." Then give him a little wink and walk away. Make sure you look flirty, but not slutty, and do everything you can to come across as sincere. If it looks like you're making fun of him, it will blow the whole thing. You might want to dress up a little bit.

I could tell you exactly why I want you to do this, but I need you to trust me. Don't ask why, just do it and see how it turns out. I promise you'll be happy with the result.

Yes, I know that no real woman would ever talk like that unless it was in a stupid story a guy who had never been kissed wrote as part of an infantile fantasy, but that's exactly why it's going to work. Yes, I know it's creepy/disgusting/gross/weird/sexist. Do it anyway.

Write after school tomorrow and tell me how it went.

Friday, March 8

That was as stupid, humiliating, and embarrassing as you promised it would be, but I did it anyway. You had better take that as a huge sign of faith. I dressed cute, right at the edge of the dress-code cliff, including the one bra in the universe that makes me look like I have a figure but that secretly wants to kill me. I even put on some makeup, which meant I had to slither out before Mom saw me because Ms. All Natural doesn't appreciate that some of us didn't inherit her looks. Bonus: I didn't want to walk all the way to school in heels so I also almost killed myself by trying to drive not wearing flats. You're welcome.

In algebra, it felt like I was some kind of dystopian government surveillance agent. I kept wanting to turn and look at Patrick during class because part of me was convinced that he knew what I was up to and it made me feel guilty for something I hadn't even done. I finally gave in and glanced at him at the end of the period so I could see what he was wearing so I wouldn't miss him later.

I almost chickened at the last minute and skipped going to my locker altogether because I'd pretty much convinced myself that I was going to either embarrass the hell out of him or make him think I was into him, but in the end I trusted you, if only because I could call you out on this being a fraud if it went badly, and because you'd berate me with it if I didn't do it at all.

Patrick was there exactly like you said he would be. He was standing with his back to the wall around the corner from where my locker is, and there were three guys facing him. I think they were seniors, but in any case they were all bigger than him and clearly got their attitude and intelligence from the monkey side of their families. Patrick always wears these nice collared shirts, and there was mud or something splattered on him that hadn't been there in class. I had to restrain myself from running—either toward him because I wanted to get it over with or away because my nerve was pretty short—and as I walked up I could hear that the dicknubs were bullying him. They were calling him "faggot" and asking disgusting things about what he liked to do with other guys and if he was into various perversions. I'm not going to write the disgusting details.

I did exactly like you said. As I walked up to Patrick, the boys stopped teasing him like I'd flipped their "go on the defensive" switch. I think they were surprised and were waiting to see what I was going to do. I put a hand on Patrick's shoulder and said I'd been thinking about last night and he should call me. I didn't wait for him to say anything, but turned and walked away. I did it on the balls of my feet to give myself a bit of an extra wiggle, which was demeaning and made me feel skanky, but I thought it was what you meant. If you were recording me for time-travel YouTube, you're a pervert and I hate you.

I heard one of the boys say, "Holy shit" or something like that, and another one said, "There is no fucking way." I didn't hear any apologies, but I glanced back before I went around the corner, and they were walking away, leaving Patrick looking kind of stunned.

After school, Patrick ran up to me just when I was leaving campus. I was in a hurry to get home because my bra was at stage three of its plan to stab me to death (having successfully passed stage two which was to give me bruises that I'll be dragging around for at least a week), plus I was really worried that this was going to be the part where I'd have to explain that I really didn't want to date him, but I think he had already figured that out for himself (the dating part, not the bra part).

Patrick walked with me for a minute, and thanked me a lot for coming to his aid (as he put it). He said he definitely owed me one, which was cool, and that he wishes he was confident and bold like me instead of feeling like he has to hide all the time. You know what? I think he might really be gay and it makes me sad to think he has to cover it up to stop assbrains from getting on him about it.

Is it weird that part of me was a little disappointed that this didn't end up with a guy being bummed when he found out I wasn't really interested in him, even though I really didn't want that to happen? I'm not unhappy with how this turned out, of course, but the fact is that I'm more than halfway through high school and have never even been on a date. Yes, I know you aren't my psychic dating service, but can you at least tell me how long I have to wait? I think I'd be able to help you better if I knew that I was heading toward a future where I have actual relationships and a normal dating life instead of just being the life partner to novels and homework. I'm worried that I'll never have a serious relationship at this rate. I don't care if it isn't any time soon, but can you just tell me how old I am when I finally lose my virginity?

No.

What I CAN do is help you get together with someone who is worth having a relationship with.

You did really well with Patrick. I hope you see that things went much more smoothly because you did exactly as I asked and didn't waste a lot of time with questions. It's really pointless for you to ask what is going to happen when you'll find out soon enough by trusting and doing. With that in mind, I'll give you another little task that will help you find a boyfriend.

I believe your history textbook is still in your backpack. Go get it. You will find that there is an advertising card stuck between the pages. Take this card with you tomorrow and leave it on your desk after English. The card should be left facedown on the lower-right corner of your desk. It doesn't have to be perfectly aligned with the edges or anything. In fact, it's better if it looks like you simply forgot it. That's all you need to do.

One other thing: you don't need to write the date on your entries. This isn't a diary. If you're hoping that I will start doing the same, put that out of your mind. It isn't going to happen.

This card is absolutely freaky! It looks like one of those pictures that changes when you tilt it. (What are those called? I don't think it's a hologram—right?) It's just white type on a black background, but however it's done it looks like the type is floating over emptiness, like the thing is a portable hole that sinks down into a forever of nothingness. It's so cool!

The card is for a place called "The Black Heart." It's on Santa Monica Boulevard, but I don't remember ever seeing it. What kind of place is that?

I also really want to know how you got the card in my book. I thought from what you said before that you couldn't send things back in time to me. Is this some kind of exception? If you can do this, then maybe you could send me notes during the day by teleporting them (or whatever) into my book while I'm at school. That would let you talk to me when I don't have the journal. I don't know how I'd send a message back, but we could think of something.

I didn't put the card in your book and I don't actually know how it got there. There are other people working toward the same goal we are, and one of them must have done it somehow. I was just told that the card would be there when the time came.

The fact that there are others at work doesn't mean that there are other people getting information from the future like you are. So far as I know, the journal we are using is ~~completely~~ unique. Anyone else aiding us has no idea what they are involved in; they are just doing little jobs or favors without knowledge of the bigger picture. I don't know who they are or how many of them there are, and it's for the best that you don't, either. There is only one other person who knows what we are doing and you will be meeting her soon.

The Black Heart is a shop specializing in the occult. It has books, jewelry, ingredients for ceremonies, and things like that. It's where Mom buys her candles and stuff. That isn't important, but I'm telling you because if I don't you might ask someone about the card or go to the shop to get answers and that would be a major distraction right now. It doesn't matter to you what the card is for. What matters is that when you leave the card as I described, it will lead you down the right path.

Be sure to leave the card at the end of the period, just as you are getting up from the desk. You should also not be in a big hurry to leave; don't even get up from your desk until you hear the room's door open behind you. Don't make a big deal out of leaving the card or pay any special attention to it, and definitely don't look back at it—just walk out of the room. You're leaving it behind accidentally. Got that?

Write tomorrow to tell me how it went.

Monday, March 11

I left the card face down on the desk after English, just
like you said. Did you know it has a weird symbol on the
back? It was some kind of funky goddess/feminist quasi-
Baphomet pentagram. I'd never seen it before, but
I didn't have time to look at it closely because I was
trying to not pay attention to the card. You keep asking
me to pretend I'm not interested in things and that's
a lot harder than you might think. I don't know how
actors do that.

There's a boy that I had never actually met before
but who I've seen around. He's a little taller than me,
blonde, and kind of tan—I think because he's on the
track team or something like that. I've only noticed
him because he's pretty handsome, and once last year
I thought he was smiling at me, but it turned out he
was looking at someone standing behind me, which was
embarrassing even though I don't think he even noticed
me. Well, when I was leaving English, he was coming
into the room and he asked if I'd forgotten something
because he saw that Olivia had picked up something
from my desk (probably because its blackness had her
gothseeking sense tingling or something).

Is it a coincidence that you keep asking me to do things
that end up involving the school's loners and outcasts, or
am I reading too much into a sample size of two?

Back to the story: I'm heading for the door when cute-guy walking in stops me and says that Olivia picked something up off my desk, looked at it, and then looked at me with a weird expression on her face. You hadn't told me what to do so I just played dumb and said I hadn't forgotten anything (which, technically, wasn't a lie). Then he got this look in his eyes and grew a little smile, like in the middle of our conversation he had literally just seen me for the first time. I asked him what the matter was and he made a nervous little jump as if suddenly remembering that reality was still going on. He said he was fine and pointed out that we were kind of blocking people coming in, so he was wondering if we could meet at lunch! I said yes without really thinking about it and we agreed to meet by the tables, but I had walked away before I realized I hadn't even asked what his name was yet.

How's that for a "meet cute"? It was so romantic!

Eric (his name) was incredibly nice at lunch. He was funny without being obnoxious and talked about himself without being braggy. He seemed really interested in what I had to say, too, and was completely without the faux-macho effect (affect?) that makes makeup-troweled blondes squeal and turns my stomach. I found out that he is indeed on the track team but that he also likes to swing dance, which is cool even though I don't really like dancing. Maybe I would if he wanted to teach me? (Insert olden-style swoon here.) His dad works for a defense contractor on honest-to-godless top-secret stuff, which is also cool, I guess, so long as it isn't military. His mother is a professor of physics at UCLA—how awesome is that! Can you believe I know so much about him already? I don't even know how I do because I feel like my mouth was on auto-blather and I didn't shut up for the whole lunch period. I think I hoped that if I didn't stop talking he wouldn't notice that 90% of my wardrobe makes me look like I'm ten. (I definitely need some new clothes.)

Lunch was over way too quick. Eric and I had this incredible automatic rapport; it was like we had known each other literally forever. He asked if we could have lunch again tomorrow. I can't even believe this is happening! How did you find him? How did you know he was so perfect for me? How did you know the thing with the card would work out like this?

I enjoy hearing about Eric. If you remember anything else be sure to tell me, even if it seems unimportant.

I'm going to ignore all of your "how" questions. At this point, you either already know the answers or already know how I'm going to answer, so there's no reason for me to waste my time. Remember that even though you have all the time in the world to write, I don't. This is a difficult and painful process for me. I want to avoid any wasted effort.

Eric is going to ask you out tomorrow. You should definitely say yes, but don't worry—I'm not going to try and micromanage your relationship with him. There may be the occasional thing I need you to do related to your romantic life, but for the most part you'll do better without my interference. Make sure to let me know how it goes.

Difficult as it may be, I need you to stop thinking about Eric for a moment and concentrate on what I'm writing. There are things you must do tomorrow and it's important that you don't let yourself be distracted. Some of these items are critical.

On your way home from school, go by the drugstore on Lincoln and buy the items on the list below. Use some of your hidden cash—you can consider this a "mad money" situation. Bring a reusable shopping bag so you don't have to pay a dime for a paper one and Mom won't freak out because you're killing trees. Don't open anything, just bring it all home. Leave everything in the bag and let me know you're back.

Here's the list:

- Security envelopes, the kind you don't have to lick
- Ream of paper
- Two cheap ballpoint pens
- Book of stamps. ~~Self-sticking, not the kind you lick.~~
- Medical exam gloves
- Athlete's foot spray
- Can of tuna you can open without a can opener
- Blue hairbrush with a square top and black bristles
- Aluminum foil
- Bag of prunes
- Razor blades
-
-
-

Did you forget that they don't make the stamps you lick anymore? I think they stopped before I was even born. Wow—if you don't even know that, you're not doing wonders for your credibility.

For someone who is supposed to know so much about me, you should also know that I already have stamps. Is your knowledge just not that detailed? Or are you saying I need a whole book of them?

The list is so random. Can you tell me what the things are for? Is it all for one job, or for a bunch of separate ones? Or are we going to build the world's lamest Rube Goldberg machine and get rich off YouTube videos? I swear that if this all ends up being some kind of pathetic future scavenger hunt I will freeze myself until I reach your time, get thawed, and end you.

The drugstore list has empty bullets, too. Do you add stuff here as things come up so I just have to make one shopping trip? If that's what you're doing, it's kind of surreal. But why put the bullets? Why not just leave blank space and then add a bullet when you need it? Do they still have obsessive-compulsive disorder in the future? What would happen if I copied your list on this page and then you went back and added something?

You'll find out what the items are for soon enough. It would be a waste of time and a complication to go into it here. As for the bullets, they're there more as a reminder to you of how things work than as an aid to me, and jokes about disabilities are offensive.

I'm not going to apologize for the mistake about the stamps. I never said that I remember everything. Things have happened to me in the past that make me less perfect than I would prefer to be. It's like I've literally got a hole in my memory that some things have fallen into. If that's a hit to my credibility, then we're both just going to have to live with it.

One thing I do remember is that you're wrong about having stamps. The book of stamps in your desk only has one left in it, and it's not even enough postage to mail a single letter. You need to buy "forever" stamps.

I don't know what would happen if you copied the list, so don't. Don't do anything that might get in my way. If I'm prevented from communicating with you because you tried to create a paradox or messed with something you don't understand, you won't like the results. I'm not threatening you because there's no way I could, but I can promise that your world will be completely torn apart without me.

That's enough for now. Get some sleep. Tomorrow, get the stuff and write to me.

How the hell did you know about the stamp in my desk? I didn't even remember about that. Or, rather, I did remember, but misremembered how many stamps I had. Did you search my room when you left the journal? Did you set up a camera in here? I was joking around with the scavenger-hunt thing but I swear, if this is some complicated perv trick I'm going to call the cops so fast you won't have time to check your ass before it's in a cell.

Forget about vague threats and "that's enough"—answers NOW!

Does my knowing about a book of stamps really sound like sufficient reason for you to burst into flames? You need to control your temper better or you're going to blow your top at a critical moment and it will lead you places that I do not want to go.

Stop being a child and use your brain for a second. I told you before that I didn't leave the journal. I also told you that I'm in the same room you are, only later. I know there's a book with a single stamp in it in your desk because it's still there, jammed in the seam in the back corner of the center drawer so even if you dumped the drawer out it would stay in place. I only noticed it when I took all the drawers out one time when I wanted to move the desk.

I was purposefully avoiding talking about who I am because I really, really was hoping we could get through this without you knowing, just to sidestep all the questions you're going to want to ask that I can't answer and avoid all the doubt that my saying who I am is going to create in your mind. I see now that there's no getting away from it because my being a "mystery woman" is just making you ask different questions and pushing you toward paranoia.

Read this whole paragraph and understand it before moving on so you don't go brainshits again: In a way, you are right about my being able to see what is in your room, but it's not because I'm watching you, it's because I am you. You are writing all the entries in this journal. You are writing to yourself.

Don't bother turning the page and writing, "That is complete bullshit." I know it sounds impossible to you because it sounds impossible to me and I know for a fact that it's true because

I remember sitting there in my chair at my desk reading this sentence and wanting to know how I know that you have only one shoe on because you slipped the other one off when the bottom of your foot started to itch. I remember thinking that there might be a camera in the room that showed you taking off your shoe and scratching it against the leg of your jeans, but that even if there was it would be impossible for anyone to write about it in the journal without you noticing since you yourself were writing in it when it happened.

I also remember that when you get to the twenty-first word in this sentence you are startled by a tiny silverfish that runs up the wall from behind the desk.

It's tempting to write some things here that only you know, but I know that putting things like that in print would make you nervous that someone might find this journal later and that would get in the way of what we need to do. So let me just say this:

- What happened when you slipped out after dark to get a ride on Pete's motorcycle
- Sneaking a look at your 13th birthday present
- Amy's second sandwich

Got that?

No more questions tonight.

Holy Fuck.

Holy fucking FUCK. That is fucking FUCKTASTIC!

You can't know those things. Those are things that have never been anywhere but IN MY HEAD.

There is no way.

This is messed up beyond anything. You can't be me. You can't be. It doesn't make any sense. But now you have to be, don't you?

I have to think about this.

I'll write tomorrow. Maybe I'll write tomorrow.

Tuesday, March 12

I'm having cereal in my room. Dad's having sausage, even though he knows I won't sit at the table when he's having murder for breakfast. I'd rather be in here writing to you anyway because there's so much to talk about.

I had a horrible time getting to sleep last night. I lay in bed for hours trying to figure out who you really were and how you were tricking me. There's no way I could believe that you're me because that's just mental, but trying to explain leaves me with nothing but impossible things to choose from. The more I thought about it the more I realized that my future self writing to me made more sense than any of the other insane possibilities. It definitely explains how you know so much about me, and if you're a lot older than me, that would explain the things you don't remember. How much do I really remember from when I was eight, or four, or two, right?

Out of all the things you said, it was the stamps that really got me. Isn't that weird? After you said I only had one and that it was old, I remembered it. And now I can imagine myself, sitting at my careworn desk, remembering what it was like to be young, and finding this old book of stamps from—how many decades back? I know you're not going to tell me so I'm not going to ask, but I'm imagining two or three. If I'm back in the house, I suppose that means that Mom and Dad are gone. You know what happened to them; I don't want to know. I had so many questions I wanted to ask you, and now I have dozens more that I'd beg you not to answer.

When you said Eric was going to ask me out, I was thrilled. I really, literally got tingling in my toes, I was so excited. It's different now. You know he's going to ask me out because you remember it happening. It's weird that should make such a big difference, but it does.

There's no thrill of waiting to see if it will really happen when I'm talking to someone who knows for a fact that it does (did?) happen.

I'm probably being too dark about this. I should probably still be excited because I know I'm going to have a nice experience today. I can still be excited about going on a roller coaster even though I know other people have been on it before, can't I? Can you believe I was depressed last night that I wasn't the first girl Eric had asked out because he'd already asked you out? That doesn't make a minispeck of sense—I'm literally jealous of myself.

You're really messing with my head. I'm messing with my head. Even that sentence was messed up. Holy fuck is this a trip.

I need time to get used to this.

I'll get through today. I'll do that shopping you told me to do. I'll write when I get home.

I am so exhausted. I don't know if I even got an hour of real sleep last night, but I think I already told you that. I can't remember if I'm allowed to look back at what I wrote before so I'm just not going to in case I might do something tired-dumb.

I take back all the stupid stuff I said this morning about not being excited about going out with Eric. I am completely jazzed about it now!

When Eric came up to me at lunch, I started giggling and couldn't stop. It was so weird that I had to wait for him to ask me out when I knew that was exactly what he was going to do, and seeing how nervous he was and how badly he was hiding it was hilarious. At least it was in that "I've been up all night so everything seems funny now" kind of way. He's got to think I'm completely insane. I wonder if he noticed I had makeup on. I think that the day I helped Patrick was the only time I've ever worn makeup at school, and Eric didn't see me then. I guess I shouldn't have worn makeup because I was only doing it because you said Eric was going to ask me out so I was only wearing makeup because of knowing what was going to happen in the future, and I guess I shouldn't do that because—what? Paradox? (Also, award for worst sentence ever: Received. Thank you.)

Apparently Eric has a thing for insane, sleep-deprived girls who sneak out of the house with makeup on because he still asked me out. We're going to the movies on Saturday. Eric asked me if I'd like to see "the new Brad Bird movie," and I said yes, even though I didn't know who that is. I still don't. I hope it's not a cartoon bird. A Muppet would be okay. Is Brad Bird a Muppet? Pardon the babbletired.

I did the shopping you asked for. Everything's still in the bag, and I'll keep it there until you tell me what to do with it.

In the meantime, considering everything I've gone through over the last day, I'm thinking that maybe you owe me one, keeping in mind that anything you do for me you're also doing for yourself. The next time you write to me, let me know what the numbers for the next lottery will be. It doesn't have to be a giant one, just $10 million or something like that. Wouldn't you have a better life now if you'd been a millionaire in high school?

We should totally help each other!

Quick tip: go to school a little early and put on makeup in the bathroom. I'm pretty sure Eric likes it, and I'm definitely sure Mom won't mind you leaving early but will notice if you start sneaking out every morning.

I could help you win the lottery but I won't. I remember when the idea came to me, lying in bed and unable to sleep. What I didn't consider was that if winning the lottery worked out I wouldn't have had to propose it. Future me would have sent back the lottery numbers right off.

This is one of those things that you have to just trust me on: if you win the lottery, things go very, very badly.

I don't want to waste a lot of pages going back and forth about this and your being tired is only going to draw things out, so I'm going to go through the next part of the conversation in shorthand.

No, we can't find some way to avoid the problems that come up because you win the lottery.

Yes, I know what the problems are, but there is no possible way around them.

There's nothing you can do to avoid them other than not play the lottery in the first place.

You might think that if I tell you exactly what will happen you can think of some clever solution, but you can't.

I am absolutely certain that anything you try is doomed to failure and we'll just end up wasting a lot of time that you don't have.

You might think that winning the lottery will change your life so much that any inconvenience is worth it, but it isn't. The project we are working on is far more important than money.

Besides, you have to be 18 to play the lottery. You couldn't buy a lottery ticket if you wanted to and you could be arrested if you tried.

I'm going back and adding this paragraph because we are wasting too much time talking about the stupid lottery. You are incredibly hard to convince and I wish you would just drop the subject. I can't believe I was so asspaining stubborn. I'm going to come right out and say it in the hope that we can move on: if you win the lottery, Mom and Dad die. You don't play it, they don't die. End of conversation.

You don't sound like me at all. I wouldn't give up so easily on something that could solve pretty much all of my family's problems. Winning the lottery will kill Mom and Dad? That's so ridiculous that even thinking I'd believe it is insulting. You're just trying to scare me away from the idea.

For a minute there you had me completely convinced you are me in the future, but I obviously have to question everything after this dick move. I don't know how you're doing it, but I think that maybe this journal is a fake and either you can't give me the lottery numbers because you aren't really in the future, or you won't give them to me because you want to keep us from getting rich or you want to win the money yourself. The other option is that you are in the future but you're afraid to give this a try because doing anything that isn't already part of your little plan interferes with your Hitlerfied control complex.

I'll tell you what: how about you give me the numbers just to prove that you really can? That might make me trust you again. I'll even promise not to use them. I just want to see if you can really do it. If you don't, then that's it. I'll know you're full of shit and I'll start turning pages in this thing until I figure out the trick.

You can't lie to yourself. If I give you the numbers, you use them and Mom and Dad die. No bullshit.

I'm not sure what to do here because I know full well how stubborn I was. You really will obstinately screw everything up if I don't give you the numbers. On the other hand, I know that regardless of my warning you will use the numbers if I give them to you because you think you're too clever to get yourself in trouble.

Here's what I'm going to do: This project is too important for me to let you derail it, so I'm going to pretend that I believe you when you say you aren't going to use the numbers. I'm going to keep trying to think of a way to stop you from breaking that promise, and when I do I'll add it earlier in this conversation. I know I've already tried that once and it didn't work, but I'm sure I can think of something if I have enough time.

Obviously I don't remember what lottery numbers were drawn on which day back then, and I can't Google it because there's no Google anymore and the remains of the internet are spotty at best. If you want the damned lottery numbers even though you're killing your parents if you use them, we're going to have to be creative about getting them to you.

On the next page, leave a couple of blank lines at the top before you start writing. The next time the lottery is drawn, go back to that page and write the winning lottery numbers in that blank space along with the drawing's date. I'll copy those numbers to the bottom of this page so that you have them before they are drawn. You will effectively be sending a message back in time to yourself.

The Powerball numbers for March 18 are 8, 14, 39, 46, 47 and Powerball 18.

The Powerball numbers for March 18 are 8, 14, 39, 46, 47 and Powerball 18.

I literally can't wrap my head around how this is supposed to work. You wrote that I should copy the numbers down on this page after the drawing, but then you had the numbers listed. I copied what you wrote to the top of this page because I think that's how this page is supposed to end up looking, but then I'm not giving you the numbers at all; you're giving them to me.

When you told me what to do, I thought I'd be filling the numbers in later, but now I realize that if I did fill them in later and you copied what I wrote, then from my perspective I'd be seeing what you copied before I wrote this page, which would change what I wrote on this page and take away my incentive for watching for the lottery numbers in the future. But what if instead of copying your writing to the top of this page I'd skipped it because I already had the numbers? Then you'd have nothing to copy on the previous page, so I wouldn't have the numbers, so I'd write them on top of this page when I got them, which would let you copy them, so I'd see them and change what I wrote here.

I suppose I should be trying to work this out to myself instead of writing it, but putting it down on paper is helping me think, I think. I think I get it now. Kind of. If I don't copy the numbers you wrote onto this page, it leads to a paradox, so the only timelines that can move forward are ones where I do copy the numbers.

Wow. I think I may actually be getting a handle on this. Or I'm so tired that bullshit seems like a delicious sandwich.

If those numbers do turn up, it will be complete proof that there really is time travel going on here. In the meantime, though, I accept your act of faith in transmitting the numbers to me and am going to put my doubts aside. I won't buy a lottery ticket. Promise. Double promise.

Amazing how your doubts evaporate when you get your way and how easily you lie when you think you can get something from it. I wish I could convince you how sorry you are going to make yourself, but I obviously can't.

There's more to do and you're too tired to do it. Go to bed for an hour. Set an alarm. When you wake up, continue reading this page.

From here on out try to get plenty of rest so you can keep focused. Don't think of me as someone who is here to help you with things. Instead, we're helping each other by your following my lead. The best way for you to help yourself is to help me. I'm looking out for our best interests.

Now that some of the edge is off your exhaustion, I need you to do some things for me.

First, regarding the things you got at the drugstore: good job not taking them out of the bag. It will be easier if we know where everything is when the time comes. For now, just take one of the razor blades out of the package and put it on the left-hand corner of your desk. It should be sitting right on the wood, uncovered, and not sticking off the edges. That's all you have to do with it. It needs to be easily available at a moment's notice later. Put the box of aluminum foil on the desk, too. When you're not writing in the journal, keep it closed with the box of foil on top of it. Go ahead and use the athlete's foot spray as indicated so that we never have to talk about your itchy stinkfeet again.

Second, when Dad gets home from the gym he's going to ask if you want to go shooting with him before dinner. Say that reminds you that you saw in the Costco mailer that they have a pallet of survival food that will last a family of four for a year. If you happen to look at the actual mailer before you talk to Dad you might notice that there's a vegetarian option; don't mention that when you talk to him. I know you don't like to encourage Dad's mild survivalist paranoia, but in this case it will do us some good.

Third, after Mom gets home from work and Dad's back from the range but not in the same room, mention to Mom that you were talking about earthquake safety at school and it got you thinking that the living room is looking a little crowded. Offer to help with packing up some of the stacks of books or moving them somewhere more out of the way. (Don't worry—she won't take you up on the offer.)

That's all for now. Don't write before you go to bed, but after you get home from school tomorrow tell me how the conversations with Dad and Mom went.

Wednesday, March 13

Sorry for yesterday's blather. I got a solid night of sleep and am going to try and be more focused from here on out.

Eric and I had lunch together again. He still likes me when I'm coherent, so that's a win! We had a long conversation and he made a bunch of jokes that were actually funny, which makes him stand out from pretty much every guy I know (including Dad; sorry, Dad). I remember us both laughing and I remember how nice it felt just to be talking with him, but I can't remember anything we talked about. Is that weird? I think it's weird. I also think that if we don't end up dating steadily I'm going to turn into his stalker. He would definitely be nice to stalk!

I can totally see myself sitting in the shadows at the base of a tree every night, gazing through his window and longing for even so much as a brush of his shadow on the curtains, and writing longingful poetry on lavender-scented stationery in ink from a fountain pen by the light of the moon before slowly tearing the sheets to confetti and sprinkling it into a passing breeze, then wandering aimlessly home in the wee hours to slip beneath the cold sheets of my bed and weep silently into my natural-fiber pillow while the pictures of him I've taped all over my headboard look down protectively on me in the darkness until I slip into sleep and dream of finding whatever bitch he's dating and stabbing her in the face.

Remind me never to let Eric read this journal.

Okay, back to business: There's not much to report from last night. I put the razor blade out like you said. Anyone coming into my room will have to decide if I'm emo, punk, a coke addict, or just into wilderness-survival-style leg shaving. I'm assuming it will make sense at some point. Moving on.

The thing with Dad was completely uneventful. He asked if I wanted to go shooting and I said no because of the gun thing on your "do not do" list. (Should I say "our" list? If you really are me, it's going to mess with our pronoun usage.) When I mentioned the Costco thing, he just said he'd take a look and that's it. I don't know if it was supposed to get him all excited or something, but it didn't.

The bit with Mom was more interesting. She told me not to worry about the books, but then later when we were waiting for dinner to be delivered she mentioned to Dad how he keeps promising to do some decluttering. Dad went on a bit about how busy he's been trying to drum up new clients, so even though he's working at home he still doesn't have a lot of free time, but he promised to at least get the books back in the office or the hall

shelves if that's where they belong, and to make a plan
to dispose of the ones he didn't need any more. He even
worked on it a bit last night and was boxing up some
books to donate to the library this morning when I left
for school. I think he was happy to have something to do
because his design business has kind of tanked.

You aren't going to tell me what the point of all this is
because blah, blah, blah, but nobody says I can't try to
figure it out myself (well, maybe you DID say that but
I'm not listening). I think there's some kind of disaster
coming that you're helping me prepare for. There are
a lot of possibilities, but I think the most likely one is
an earthquake. You want to convince Dad to clean up
so we don't run into obstacles when trying to escape,
and talking about survival stuff will keep him in the
right state of mind for when it happens. I think the
razor is for me to protect myself. Maybe after the
earthquake there's riots or looting and I have to help
fight off a home invasion? That sounds terrifying—more
like a situation for one of Dad's guns than for a razor,
but I think that if I try to use a gun on the invaders
something happens and they get it away from me.
That's why I need to have the razor.

I don't know if I could actually cut someone, even in an
emergency. I guess if I was pushed too hard, maybe.
I'm not sure. You'd definitely know better than I would!

Stop it. Don't speculate. It's a stupid, pointless, child's game. You aren't going to guess what's going on and I'm not going to even react to speculation until I'm completely sure that telling you won't make things worse. Haven't I made clear enough that this is difficult for me and that we only have limited time and resources to get this done? No more telling stories. When you have the big picture, you're going to look back on what you just wrote and be embarrassed for yourself. It's pathetic how narrow you think the world is. You think you're such a

Ignore that. I'm running low on medication and it's keeping me on edge. Please don't do any more speculating. It isn't helpful and might lead you down an incorrect path. Just trust me and see where things go.

I will say that your guess about the razors being weapons is a step in the right direction. If you think about killing, think about razors. If you think about hurting someone, think about razors. Work on keeping that association live in your mind and you'll be more sure to make the right choice when the time comes. You can definitely work up the will to try and kill someone if pushed hard enough, but if all goes well you won't need to go there. Enough about that for now.

The tasks I have for you today are very specific and a bit more unusual than what we've done before. Once again they are going to make you a little uncomfortable, but you need to do them anyway. Don't allow your discomfort to distract you from following my directions precisely.

It's grocery day and it's also Coven Wednesday. Dad's been procrastinating on doing errands, so he's going to have to go to the store after dinner while Mom gets ready to go to

Coven. There are two things you need to do while Mom takes a shower and gets dressed, so you are only going to have about 20 minutes to do them.

The first thing you need to do is find Dad's old diabetic testing kit. When he got his implant, he put it in the bag with the first-aid stuff in the hall closet. Take it with you to the kitchen, get a soup spoon, and then go to the back room and get Mom's traveling kit—the wooden toolbox/case thing Mom takes with her to Coven—from under the spirit altar. Keep it on the ground and sit next to it, then open it and pull out the top drawer. There is a set of bottles marked with planetary symbols on their stoppers. Get the one with the Mars symbol, put it on the ground, and remove the stopper.

Dad's testing kit has that stabby thing that you put sterile lancets into so you can prick your finger to do a blood test. Get that and load one of the lancets. This next part is particularly weird but do it anyway: Hold the stabby thing in your right hand, kiss the pad of the ring finger of your left hand, lick the pad of that finger, and then use the stabby thing to puncture the finger right in the middle of the pad. It's going to hurt, so be ready for that. Put down the stabby thing and use your right hand to squeeze your left ring finger below the puncture until you can get a drop of blood to fall into the bottle you opened. Suck on your finger to clean it off (you'd normally want to keep it sterile and put a bandaid on it, but don't worry about it; you don't get infected). Put the stabby thing back in its pouch. Stopper the bottle, put it back where it was, and close the drawer but don't close the box.

Below the drawer with the bottles is a drawer with boxes. Open it and find the box with the Pisces symbol. Take it and the spoon into the back yard. Open the box, take note of how full it is, and dump the dirt that's in it behind the bushes by the door. Go to where you buried Boxtop and use the spoon to dig a small hole about three inches deep. Dad planted Boxtop about six inches down, so you don't have to worry about running into turtle bones. Replace the dirt that was in the box with an identical amount of dirt from the bottom of the hole you just dug. Be sure to just get dirt and not rocks or anything else.

Close the box. Fill in the hole. Go back in the house. Replace the box in the case and close it all up. Put the case back under the altar. Rinse the spoon off in the sink and put it in the dishwasher. Put the testing kit back where you found it.

Done.

Read that over a few times to make sure you have it all. Remember, you have enough time to do it, but just barely, and you can't forget anything.

Mom is going to wake you up when she gets home from Coven. When she does, write and tell me what happens.

Let's see here, you want me to sneak around behind my mother's back, pollute ingredients that she is power-obsessed about keeping pure, dig in a beloved pet's grave, and stab myself with an old needle, all with the precision timing of a bank-heist movie, no questions asked. Gosh, is that all? #noproblem

This is going to be the biggest act of faith ever. I'm in serious trouble if I'm caught and I have some major reservations about messing with Mom's magic stuff. Also: creepy.

I know it's supposed to be all for the best and blah blah, but the payoff is going to have to be pretty spectacular if you're ever going to convince me to do something like this again. I'll be stressed out all afternoon until Mom takes her shower.

Hang on a second. I thought we agreed that Mom's coven was a bunch of kids playing with an unplugged Easy Bake oven? She's like a middle-age Olivia, still Goth at 40 but desperately trying to convince herself that it means something. But if you want me to change the ingredients that she's—I presume—going to use at Coven tonight, that implies that they're actually doing magic, doesn't it? I love Mom, and I'd never say anything to her face, but I always thought her witchcraft thing was an adorable eccentricity at best and another religion as pointless as any other at worst. But if in the future

I think something will happen if they use different ingredients, then that means that I end up believing in that stuff, doesn't it?

My first reflexive thought was that I eventually go off my rocker and get all woo. Then I realized I was thinking that because I've been talking to my future self using a magic book. Maybe I do believe in magic already, just a little bit. Given the evidence, maybe I don't have a choice.

I wish I knew what the new ingredients were supposed to do. Hair and blood are used to bind things to you or to control them, but blood can also be used to give a spell life force or control a person's life force. The giving-life-force thing makes the most sense because there's no reason for the Coven to do a spell that has anything to do with me, unless that's what you're secretly trying to get them to do. Graveyard dirt is for grounding, expressing mortality, or—one other thing. Connecting to the planet? Or is that just dirt in general? Mom used to tell me all this stuff before she gave up in the face of unrelenting disinterest.

I know that I would never hurt Mom and I doubt that would ever change, so whatever it is we're doing, it isn't some kind of nasty trick on her. We're just plugging in their oven a bit, right? Mom has always said that they just do their ceremonies to invoke good magic and help people, so if it actually works for once, that's not a bad thing. Right?

I think I'm blathering because I'm nervous. Messing with Mom's personal stuff bothers me even more than the thing about bleeding myself. I'll do it, though, and I'll write tonight.

Remember: Spectacular.

_____ Thursday, March 14

It's almost three in the morning. I thought you meant that Mom was going to come into my room and wake me when she got home, but instead she was whooping and laughing so much that she woke me up. I went into their bedroom, the light was on, and Mom was practically dancing around the bed. She still had her skyclad robe and sandals on and Dad was sitting up in bed, trying to break out of sleep and figure out what was going on.

When she finally calmed down enough to make the slightest bit of sense, Mom said the coven had experienced some kind of breakthrough. They were doing a Sacrifice of Sorrows, dedicating one of the circle's will to bettering her fortune, and when they touched the flame to the bowl, instead of the little flame of the flash paper igniting atop their mixture, they got an unearthly bright light. She said it was like a window to the sun had opened up in their bowl, sending a column of blinding heat into the sky. Instead of going up into infinity, the light curved back down toward town. She couldn't see where it hit because they were in the trees, but there was no way that natural light could have curved like that.

Mom was pretty sure that what made the difference was a new ceremonial bowl that one of the other women had bought over the weekend. Apparently, Mom had seen it in a shop and been so impressed that it was both hand-carved from local stone and explicitly intended for sorrow collection that she would have bought it herself if it wasn't so expensive. This other woman bought it as a surprise for the group after hearing Mom describe it. The bowl was black with butterflies carved around the rim, but she didn't have any other details about it. If it's important, I can ask.

After telling me all about the ceremony, Mom kind of grinned at Dad with this look that no kid wants to see on their mother's face. It left emotional scars all the Brillo pads in the universe won't be enough to scour out of my head, but a near-fatal scrubbing might be worthwhile if it stopped me from having to think about what they did after she chased me out of their room.

Desperately trying to change the subject: There's something I want to ask you about. It's hard for me to say for sure because she was grinning so much the whole time, but I think Mom had fewer wrinkles at the corner of her eyes than normal. She definitely didn't have the gray at her roots that she had this morning, and I know for a fact that she wasn't in the shower long enough to have done her hair (believe me, I was keeping very close track of how long she was in the shower today). Could she really have changed, or am I so wound up that I'm seeing things or not thinking straight? I really need you to tell me. Mom has always said that youth magic is tied to vanity so it's something that only dark-arts practitioners evoke. Now that I have to believe this stuff is real, do I have to start worrying about Mom being involved in black magic?

Please tell me right now. I'm going to read one page and then I really have to go back to bed.

There's no black or white magic any more than there is good or evil electricity. You can pass a law to save the poor or enrich the wealthy. You can use a gun to murder or stop a murder. A baby can be brought up to be Hitler or Taylor Swift. All magic is of one substance, so it's a matter of what you do with it, not of what it is.

Mom is sadly innocent when it comes to magic—in the next few months you're going to learn more about it than she's picked up in her whole life—but she's a good person at heart. It would never enter into her mind to do something evil with supernatural power, even if she had it, which—despite what happened tonight—she doesn't.

After we're done with our work and you have more free time, you're going to find some old boxes of Grandma Kay's stuff in the attic crawl space. There are some diaries that talk about things when Mom was little. One of them describes Mom training a squirrel to jump into and out of a coffee can, which Grandma thought was a sign that Mom might have a talent for animal magic, but Mom was more interested in what Grandma called "hippie magic"—whatever that meant. The point is, if Mom ever did have magical talent, she apparently didn't pursue it in a way that would help her truly develop it, at least according to Grandma.

Sorry—I shouldn't have wasted our time going there. None of that is important right now.

What happened at Coven is a very good sign. I don't know what the light was exactly, but the fact that it appeared means that you did everything right. Mom really did get a little younger, but that was just a side effect of the energy release. It happened to her whole coven, but most of them won't notice right away because the change is smaller for everyone else (they weren't as close to the light as Mom). What's important is that we helped the coven create real magic, and that it was powerful enough to draw our world and another a tiny fraction closer together. More about that when the time is right.

Tonight was a major hurdle for me. Even though I remember it working out perfectly, it still made me nervous until I read your description of events. I know that isn't rational, but then who is?

There is one thing I need you to do for me tomorrow. It's not something I want you to do, but I have to ask you to do it anyway. I'm sorry.

Tomorrow when you go to school, take the can of tuna that you bought at the drugstore with you. On the way home, when you get to the corner of Euclid, pop the top off the can and carry it. You can drop the lid in a trash can when you pass one. Carry the open can of tuna in your hand all the way home. At some point, a brown cat with a white ear is going to start following you. Don't stop for it or pet it, just let it follow you. When you get to the house, walk around to the back yard instead of going in the house. Put the can of tuna in the grass next to the wall. The cat will eat it, but you don't have to wait for that or do anything else. Just go in the house, tell Dad a cat followed you home and is in the back yard, and go about your usual after-school business.

Because it was after midnight when I wrote the last time, I should have put the date after the break to show it was the beginning of a new day. I didn't realize it until after I read your response, then I turned back and added the date without giving it any thought, like I would do if I forgot to put my name on a test. Now I'm worried that my adding to what I wrote might cause some kind of weird problem. To you, the date would have been there all along, but if you noticed that I wrote it on the break line instead of after it, what then? I don't know. I'm trying really hard not to think about the mechanics of this thing because there's enough in the world that makes sanity an endangered species without going out of my way to add something else.

Great—now I want to go back and cross it out because I'm not supposed to erase anything. Wait, is it me who isn't supposed to erase things or you who can't erase things? Or both? Fuck it. If you're dead or the alien invasion succeeded or Mom's coven's "Portal to Everlasting Peace" spell collapsed or I stub my toe or whatever because I went back and wrote the date, well, shit.

Mom and Dad were still asleep when I left for school. I don't even want to think about why because gross. Thank godless Mom never has classes or office hours the morning after Coven or she'd be late for work for the most embarrassing reason ever. Could you imagine trying to explain to your boss, "Sorry I'm late, but last night magic lights shaved five years off my life and made me really horny"? Great—now I hate myself for writing that.

I tried the thing where I went to school early and put on makeup in the bathroom. I guess it's better than sneaking around, but the school bathroom mirrors are so spotty and the lighting so bad that they make me look like the undead host of a blackhead convention. You also didn't remind me to bring makeup remover, so instead of sneaking out I had to sneak in, but at least only Dad was home.

Eric and I had lunch again. I think it's officially our thing now! This time, he'd left a note in my locker that I found when I put in my books. It was in a small envelope and printed with a fancy handwriting font like a formal invitation, asking for the pleasure of my company at 11:30. It even had a little "RSVP" card that I filled out and stuck in his locker (accepting; obv). He even paid for my lunch and acted like one of the benches was our reserved table. We pretended like it was a big date until the bell rang, which was the stupidest/wonderfullest thing I've ever done. Crap—does this mean that Saturday is going to be our second date? Or our first "official" date? I think today should count as our first date so that it will be a cute story to tell when people ask about when we first went out.

Now I'm making plans for reminiscing about a relationship that's not even a week old. Why don't I just name our kids right now and get that out of the way? (I'm thinking Empress and Malik—right?)

The only hint of shade was in the little bit of not-currently-with-Eric sadness right after lunch. I started thinking about what you said about the Coven "drawing another world closer." What's up with that? Is it as creepy as it sounds? You're lucky that Eric has the magic ability to make me not worry about stuff so much or I wouldn't have been able to put it out of my mind so easily.

I floated through the rest of the day and did the cat thing on the way home. What was the point of that? After the sneaking around, self-stabbing, and exploding, it was kind of a letdown. The cat's hanging out in the backyard now and I think I permanently smell like cheap, sitting-on-the-drugstore-shelf-since-2003 canned tuna. I can't think of what that gets us, except for maybe fleas.

I'll tell you what I know about other worlds. There's something called the "plane of separation" that stands between our world and a completely different one. That world has energies that are completely inaccessible on our world and can be used to do all sorts of wonderful things. Grandma Kay worries some about it in her diary, mostly when discussing things that should never be done because they might touch the plane. She had been taught that the things beyond the plane were evil, but they aren't. At least, they aren't any more evil than the weather. As it was explained to me, anyone who thinks an earthquake is evil is just using "evil" as a synonym for "thing I don't like." At worst the things on the other side of the plane are as uncaring about morality as a rainstorm, and whether you feed or drown a baby with the water that falls from the sky has nothing to do with the clouds being good or evil. The plane's not bad, just disinterested and alien, no matter what Grandma was taught by people who were too afraid of things they didn't understand to try to learn more about them.

If you have any more questions about that, hold onto them. You're going to meet someone later who will be happy to set your mind completely at ease about them.

There are other tasks like the cat thing that you are going to need to do even though they seem completely disconnected from our overall plan. They are not about having a direct effect, but about creating ripples that will grow into something important in the future.

Come back tonight after dinner. There's something you need to do for tomorrow.

Important ripples? So far, they're the most boring super-important ripples ever.

A woman came by at around nine looking for the cat. I think Dad found the number on its collar and called her to come get it. With all of your mysterious evasiveness and talk about magic I keep expecting weird, spooky stuff to happen, but this one was a major letdown. The woman was mid-twenties and had that "I'm a yoga instructor on the side when I'm not shopping at Whole Foods" look that inspires me to punch people. I only saw her for a minute when Dad went into the yard to get the cat and pretty much just smiled at her on my way to my room because I wasn't sure if I was supposed to talk to her or not. Too bad because she could probably give me some "how not to look so much like the unpopular girl in a sitcom" tips.

Lucky for me I didn't try to talk to her because it turns out she has the conversational restraint of the Home Shopping Network. She and Dad stood in the front hall and talked for almost an hour about gun control of all things. I could overhear them pretty well and got to hear something as rare as dodo McNuggets: Dad agreeing that maybe there was a place for some limited restrictions on gun ownership. The woman didn't say anything I haven't said a hundred times back before giving up talking to Dad about having a clue where guns are concerned, so I think it was less the force of her arguments and more the magic of megacleavage. It's embarrassing how much of a guy Dad can be at times.

While we're on the subject of boobage, the folks on the other side of that plane wouldn't happen to know any magic that would remind puberty that it left a job half finished around here, would they? Just asking.

The woman and her cat finally left when Mom came out of the office to see what all the chatting was about. After the front door closed, I think I could actually hear the look she gave Dad.

Despite my ranting, the woman (I think her name was Amy?) was actually pretty nice. I'm interested to see what part she (I'm assuming) plays in the big plan you won't tell me about.

~~I wish the "nice" cat lady had gotten hit by a fu~~

Don't think about the woman any more. I'm not entirely sure, but I think that if the cat hadn't followed you home, then at some point in the next week the house would be broken into and you and Dad would be murdered. Because of the cat, you'll be safe. Leave it at that.

I can't stand the constant reminders of what a child I was. Stop hinting that you want to know more; I'm telling you everything you need to know. Stop talking about your looks; you're never going to be beautiful. If you want to know something about the future, I'll tell you that you end up looking pretty goddamned horrible and it's your own fault because when it came right down to it the one time you didn't listen to me was the one time it made the most difference. We aren't going to let that happen this time around, though, are we?

It's time to get to work. Put that other shit out of your head and follow these instructions very carefully. This is a lynchpin moment. You get this wrong and it's all for nothing. Got that?

Get the bag with the stuff you bought at the drugstore. Take out the medical gloves and put a pair on. Don't touch anything else in the bag until you have the gloves on and don't take the gloves off until you are instructed to. It's going to make everything difficult, but you need to live with that.

Get the paper and pens you bought. Take out a single sheet of paper and slowly, deliberately write your complete address in large block letters right in the middle of it. Take your time, making sure all of the lines are as straight and clean as you can make them. If you don't think it's going well, you can start over on another piece of paper, but if you do that you need to burn or shred the paper you abandoned right after you're instructed to take the gloves off.

When you have your address written, fold the paper in thirds. Get one of the security envelopes and address it using the same clean, deliberate characters you used on the piece of paper. Address it to:

> Sinclair Morsten
> c/o General delivery
> Malibu, CA 90263

The same instructions go for destroying any envelopes you write on but don't use.

Put the folded letter in the envelope, seal the envelope after making sure that no hairs or anything else fell in it, and put two stamps on it at 45-degree angles so they look like a pair of diamonds in the corner.

Put the sealed envelope in your backpack, then take off the gloves and put them in a different pocket of the backpack.

Tomorrow on the way to school, change your route so that you pass by the post office. When you're a block away, get out the gloves and put them on, and then get out the letter so you're carrying it when you pass the post office. Drop it in a mailbox. After you've walked another block, take off the gloves and drop them in the trash can by a bus stop.

Read those instructions twice and be sure you carry them out flawlessly. Write when you get home from school.

I take it you aren't particularly fond of Amy and that I turn into kind of a touchy bitch in my old age. I guess the tree doesn't grow far from the seed, or whatever. Maybe if I make a point of avoiding her she won't have a chance to do whatever it is that ends up making me so pissed at her. Of course, I could taunt you by saying that maybe if I spent a lot of time with her and built up a nice, friendly relationship everything might turn out peachy-keen this time around, but I think it's probably in my long-term best interest not to do anything that might make you go hissyfit again.

That was some pretty dodgy shit you asked me to do with the letter. Are we spies, kidnappers, conspiracy theorists, or just paranoid? I tried Googling Sinclair Morsten but didn't find anything. All kidding aside, if you aren't going to tell me what the letter was for, can you at least reassure me that it wasn't somehow something criminal? I don't know how it could be, but all the CSI precautions against fingerprints and what have you made me nervous. I can't see how sending someone my address could be any kind of threat. All I can think of is that I was telling someone where to find me, but I don't know who that could be. Will you warn me if someone is going to be looking for me?

Sorry about going off on you. I'm having a rough time and you're right about her being a touchy subject. Believe me when I say that trying to be her friend would only make things much, much worse down the road.

The business with the letter is complicated but not immoral. I would definitely tell you if there was someone or something you had to watch out for, or if there was something you had to be prepared to do. Right now, the razor is the only contingency you have to worry about and I'll let you know exactly when you need to use it. Remember: If I put you in danger, I put me in danger.

Tomorrow, Mom and Dad are going to go out. I think they were going to Santa Barbara to visit the business of a potential client for Dad and then go out to dinner or something like that. The details don't matter; you need to stay home. If they ask you to go with them, make an excuse about schoolwork or something.

A package is going to be delivered on Saturday. You won't have to talk to the man who brings it. He'll just leave it and go. After he does, bring it inside immediately. You shouldn't have the opportunity to, but even if you do, don't show it to anyone and don't tell anyone about it. Don't open it. Write when you have it.

No, you can't leave it like that. Why can't I open the package? That means it's either something dangerous or something scary, right? I think it has to be a magic ingredient of some kind. Hemlock? A human skull? Dragon bits? Famous underwear? Am I getting close?

I'm trying to sound jokey but this really is going to bother me. If it's going to be something alive in there that you don't want to escape, or something that could explode or leak acid, I really want to know. I can handle whatever it is, but I can't handle not knowing what it is. It will make me too nervous. I'm going to spend all night dreaming that I open the package and something jumps out and Aliens my face, or it's full of dead roaches, or I ruin Christmas. Come on, give me something!

I don't remember being that nervous. More precisely, I don't remember your today very well at all. You do a lot tomorrow, so today pales in comparison so much that I've let it slip away to almost nothing.

That means that nothing bad happens, because if it did, I'm sure I'd remember it. Take some comfort in that.

There's nothing dangerous or horrifying in the package. The reason you can't open it is that if you do, you're going to want to keep what's inside, but you can't do that. It's not for you. You might think that you could take a little piece of it and nobody would notice, but that's not the case at all and I know for a fact that the temptation would be intense. If you don't take the package where it needs to go unopened and completely intact, very, very, very bad things happen. There is no way I can emphasize this enough. Stick seven more "verys" in there. Tomorrow is important, and that package is the centerpiece of it all.

I know that my saying all this is just going to make you more curious. Think about this: After you tell me you have the package, I'm going to tell you where to take it. Once you take it there, you're going to give it to someone very important and she's going to open it. You'll get to see exactly what's inside. The more quickly you follow directions, the more quickly you'll see what all the fuss is about.

Don't write again until after the package has arrived.

Again ☺

Saturday, March 16

The "again" was my lame attempt to get revenge on you for the world-record-setting anticlimax that was just delivered. The truck arrived with the year's worth of emergency food Dad ordered from Costco. It was an enormous pile of boxes shrink-wrapped to a palette. I had the delivery guys put it in the garage because there was no way I was going to even try to move it myself, no matter what you said. It would have taken all afternoon.

I know you said not to open it, but it isn't exactly a surprise. The boxes are labeled and I had to sign an invoice receipt thing. Which brings up another point— you said I wouldn't have to talk to anyone, but I had to answer all these questions about where to put it and can I sign for it. You were seriously off your game this time, Miss "I'd remember if there was something important to remember." Let's hope you didn't forget anything more significant than the fact I'd be annoyed at you for working me up over nothing.

The "don't let anyone else know" thing is also out the window. Dad knew the delivery was coming and before they left he showed me where in the garage to have them put it. I had to work hard not to look surprised when he told me to expect a delivery. Was he not supposed to know? How could it possibly be a secret from him when he was the one who ordered it in the first place?

Dad ordered the vegetarian option, by the way. When I talked to him about the survival food, you told me not to mention the vegetarian thing, and I bet that if I had he would have chosen the slaughterhouse version because he's always automatically gotten defensive when I talk about cruelty-free eating. It's kind of sweet that left to his own thoughts he chose the option I can eat because he wants me to be safe during a disaster and obviously he and Mom will be just fine with vegetarian, freeze-dried, astronaut-style, blandcrap survival rations.

Now we come to the exciting part where you give me instructions for delivering this stuff and tell me a) how the heck I'm going to get it there, and b) how I'm going to convince Dad that it never arrived, was stolen, etc.

THAT'S NOT THE PACKAGE!

Stop journaling and go wait for the real delivery. You CANNOT risk missing it!

Got it!

This is much more like what I expected. Sorry about the Costco misfire. It wouldn't have happened if you'd told me I was getting two deliveries. Maybe I was supposed to figure it out myself because the Costco delivery was entirely different from what you described, but everything that we've been doing is so weird I feel like I just have to accept anything that happens. It isn't my fault if we're too dumb to explain things to myself correctly. Or whatever.

The package is small, maybe six inches on a side, and wrapped in every direction with duct tape—you can barely see the cardboard peeking through. It's so heavy that the guy who delivered it used a handcart to get it to the doorstep. He was real dodgy, too, driving a dirty white pickup truck that looked like an extra from the Cars version of Walking Dead and wearing sunglasses, a baseball cap, and an expression I couldn't see because he just stared at his feet the whole time. I watched him through the window and waited for him to knock on the door, but he never did. He just left the package and took off.

I could barely get it in the door before I had to put it down again. Did someone send me a black hole wrapped in lead-covered uranium? After all the buildup I really want to open this thing! What do I do now?

You'll strain your back if you try to carry the box through the house, so get Dad's office chair, put the box in the seat, and roll it to the garage. Put the box in the trunk of your car.

After you put Dad's chair back, text Mom and tell her that you were invited to Eric's house to study and that she doesn't need to worry because his parents are home. Let her know you're going to have dinner there before going on your movie date.

You're going to take the package to The Black Heart. That's the shop from the advertising card you had earlier. If you don't remember where it is, it's in your phone's maps search history from when you looked up the address on the card.

When you get to the shop, park at a meter right in front of the door. You're going to have to circle the block a couple of times, but you won't be able to carry the box farther than that.

In The Black Heart, put the box on the floor by the counter next to the cash register. DO NOT put the box on the counter. Yes, that would be easier, but the counters are glass and you don't want to risk an embarrassing accident.

Melissa, the owner of the shop, will be there. She's white, a little taller than you, and has long, straight brown hair. She'll be wearing a black, button-up blouse with the first few undone so you can see a bit of a butterfly tattoo on her chest. If there's anyone in the shop other than her, stand next to the box and wait. Once you are alone, Melissa will come over and just say, "Yes?" When she does, you say, "I've come to trade the box you ordered for tomorrow's journal." Make sure you say EXACTLY that.

Melissa will tell you what to do from there. Whatever she does or says, don't question her. You can always ask me about things later. I cannot emphasize enough how intimidating Melissa can be. Prepare yourself for that and keep your wits about you—you're going to be tempted to be smarmy in reaction to how tense she makes you feel, but don't go there. If there's one person you want to make a good impression on, this is her.

After you're done, come home and write to me to tell me how it went. You'll go to Eric's after that.

I hate to delay this even one minute, but it feels wrong to text Mom that I'm going to Eric's. If I do that, then I'm going to have to convince him to say that I visited in case someone asks and I really don't want to ask him to lie. I also really don't want to tell him about the journal—I'm sure you don't want me to tell him about it, either—but I also don't want to tell him a lie. Do you remember how much I like this guy? I know I've only really known him for less than a week, but there's something really special here. I wish you'd tell me how it turns out between us because I'd be thrilled to know if it works out, but if it doesn't I won't feel like such an idiot when it happens if I haven't been doing girly blather about him in my diary. I know you won't tell me, so don't even say it.

Here's another idea. Mom and Dad said they wouldn't be home until late and it doesn't sound like trading the box for the journal is going to take that long. Maybe I could just text that I'm going to go out and do some errands but stay vague about it? I assume your concern is that they might call when I'm out and wonder where I am, but they always call my cell phone anyway. If they really wanted to, they could use the app that shows them where I am, which is another reason I don't think I should lie about where I'll be. It's just too easy for them to find out, and if I turn my phone off so they can't track me, it would look

Hang on—I just got a text from Eric asking if I could come over this afternoon to study because his parents said he has too much homework so he's not going to be allowed to take me to the movies tonight. I texted back yes, then texted Mom about the change in plans. How the hell did you do that? I hadn't even finished writing this page yet when he texted. Or did you already know he'd ask me and just forget to mention it? Whatever—I'm on my way to drop off the package with my anti-intimidation shield on.

That was such an unbelievable weirdpile that I don't know where to start, so I'm going to be uncreative and chronological.

It took me twice around the block before the spot right in front of Black Heart opened up. You were definitely right to tell me to wait for that. I barely got in the door without dropping the box. Thank Nobody the counter is so near the front of the store.

There was a couple—a man and a woman—talking to (who I assumed was) Melissa over a showcase in the back of the store. The man didn't say anything the whole time they were there but was so pale that I thought he was going to throw up. The woman looked like she'd been crying and was talking to Melissa very quickly in a whisper so harsh I couldn't understand a word even though I wasn't more than 20 feet away. When the woman paused, Melissa said, "There's nothing to be done." The woman raised a hand and for a second I thought she was going to slap Melissa, but then her expression fell like she'd suddenly realized that if she went ahead with it she'd be leaving her hand in the store. She dropped her stillborn slap, let out a horrible sob, and ran past me, out of the store, pouring tears. The man who was with her looked hopelessly at Melissa and just walked out.

The woman had left her purse behind on the showcase. Melissa picked it up, wrapped the strap around the bag, and just casually tossed it into a cardboard box behind the counter on her way over to me. She gave me a tolerant little smile and said, "Yes?" just like you said she would, but the way she said it made me feel like I was in first grade coming to admit to the teacher that I'd done something wrong when she knew exactly what I'd done and what I was about to say.

Melissa's whole attitude really threw me. She can't be older than—what? 24? But an air of superiority was pouring off of her in waves so strong that it felt completely justified. When I tried to talk, it was like I was a wounded antelope asking a hungry lioness if she could spare some change for a cup of coffee. That's why I said the first thing that came out of my mouth instead of what I was supposed to say. I said, "What was wrong with that woman?"

Melissa's smile got a tiny bit bigger and was all the more imposing for how genuine it was. She said, "She couldn't mind her own business so her husband's going to die."

I wasn't sure if that was the truth, a horrifyingly bleak joke, or a barely veiled threat, but it was enough to snap me back on track. I said the thing about bringing a box to trade for the journal. Melissa asked for the box and held out her left hand like I was going to hand her a ring box. I almost warned her about the box's weight, but then I remembered you said not to question her and frankly I thought that if I made her look like an idiot by handing her a half ton of whatever, that might not be such a bad thing for my quickly evaporating ego.

I squatted down, picked up the box in both hands while making a conscious effort not to grunt despite my being very tired of lifting the damned thing, and put it right square center in her smooth, perfectly manicured, black-fingernail-polished hand. I don't know how well you remember this woman, but at a glance you wouldn't take her for someone who exercised more than was necessary to maintain a nice figure. That's why I assumed the box was going to flatten her hand against the counter like a flapjack under a car jack. Instead, her hand didn't move an inch when I gave her the box, I shit you not. She didn't even change expression. The only sign that this was anything but a box of feathers she was holding was the muscles on her arms, which suddenly looked like a bag of steroid-hyped pythons. I swear, from the looks of her biceps, she must be bench pressing people who were bench-pressing bench pressers.

She set the box gently on the counter and—again, not even the slightest amount of shitting going on here—sliced through the duct tape with her GOD DAMNED FINGERNAIL! She opened the box, cleared a few layers of thickly folded newspaper, and then started to pull out a bunch of white plastic tubes. There were a few dozen at least.

When the tubes were all on the counter, Melissa cleared the rest of the newspaper out of the box and opened one of the tubes. It was filled with bright gold coins— twenty five or so. They didn't look like anything I had ever seen before. They were flawless, like they'd never been touched, and had a picture of a deer on one side and a bearded guy (Charles Darwin?) on the other. When the tube was empty, she gave the coins on the counter the first complete smile I'd seen from her, scooped them up in her hands, and set them into the box. Then she went through the tubes, opening each one, pouring its coins into the box, and throwing the tube into the trash under the counter.

Let me take a break from describing here to point out that at no point did Melissa count these coins. She just dumped them in the box like stereotype-Grandpa's collection of unsorted pennies, and when she was done, she closed the box and stuck it on a shelf behind her as if it was no big deal. If you hadn't made such a big point of my not opening the box, I definitely could have taken one or two and she never would have noticed. Do you know how much that would have meant to me? Do you remember how many financial problems we were having back when you were my age? A gold coin has to be worth thousands of dollars, and a few of those would have made a big difference. Maybe you need to loosen up a bit and let me make some of my own decisions about how much risk is acceptable. I promise to listen if you say things are going to go bad, but let's not rule out options just because you're too risk-paranoid to try them.

I also think I deserve a better view of the big picture. If you had this plan for getting a box full of gold, why couldn't I have just kept it? What could you possibly want to do with this journal that is worth more than a box full of gold? What could Melissa do for us that is more valuable than the contents of that box? Thinking of the opportunity you made me throw away is going to bug me for a long time. You really need to consider my circumstances more, and if you don't remember what it's like, ask me.

Rant over. Back to the story.

There was an old paperback book on the counter, and after she'd put the box on the shelf Melissa slid it over to me. "That's for you," she said.

"Is this the journal?" I asked.

"It's a gift. For your trouble," is all she said.

I hesitated a bit there, caught between not questioning and not knowing what to do. "Aren't you supposed to give me the tomorrow journal?" I asked.

"I already did," she said. "More than a week ago. Under your pillow."

I just stood there, deer-in-headlights dumb, until she said, "Is there anything else?"

I said no, thanked her, picked up the book, left, and came home.

I got a parking ticket, by the way. You didn't include "put change in the meter" in my instructions, and I was so busy trying to remember what I was supposed to do that I didn't think about it. That's going to be a fun conversation when the bill from the city comes.

The book she gave me was a paperback of short stories by Shirley Jackson. We read one of them last year in English, and it was okay. I looked in it to see if there was some kind of message, or maybe if it was hollowed out and had a secret compartment, but it was normal except for an inscription written on the title page. It was signed from my mom to my dad, in her handwriting, two years before I was born, and said, "For my demon lover," which is gross.

I'd never seen it before, at least not that I remember. It had to be Melissa's way of proving that she'd been in the house. That explains how the journal got here and maybe how the card got in my textbook, but it's freaky. She wasn't the most pleasant person to be around, and knowing that she can get in and out of the house without leaving any sign makes me shiver like I'm being watched. For a second I thought that maybe it was her sneaking in and writing the responses to my writing in this book, but obviously that's impossible since I don't have to leave the journal alone for the responses to be there.

You had better be going to tell me where all that gold came from. I don't think there's a secret address where if you mail them a letter they automatically send you fabulous riches. You said there are other people working, but unless one of them is a moneychucking leprechaun, the gold was either stolen or somebody traded one hell of a favor for it. I need you to untuck your talk hole a bit and reassure me that this isn't going to come back and bite me in the ass.

Doing the errand and writing this took longer than I expected. Eric is going to be here in half an hour to pick me up to go to his place. I think that's enough weird for one day, but I'll read your response in case you actually want to answer my questions or there's anything else on your crazy to-do list.

You're right that there are other people at work. You're also right that I'm not going to tell you where the gold came from. You'll know soon enough, but it would just be a distraction now. Be assured that your ass is perfectly safe.

Regarding your wanting to keep the gold: without the gold there would be no journal, and without the journal there would be no gold. The only futures in which you get the journal are those in which you give Melissa the gold. All of it. She is much more meticulous than it might seem and would have instantly known if something was missing. If you work with Melissa, are honest with her, and don't try to get in her way, she can be a powerful ally, particularly if there's something you can do for her. But if you try and mess with her you will absolutely end up with the short, burning, poisoned end of the pointy stick stuck right in your eye.

There is one more thing for tonight. When you're at Eric's, I need you to excuse yourself for a minute, go to the upstairs bathroom, and take the hairbrush that's in the drawer to the left of the sink. Wrap it in toilet paper and put it in your purse. Leave the brush that you got at the drugstore in its place. They should look enough alike that nobody is likely to notice.

Don't worry about the ticket. You don't need to pay it and there won't be a bill from the city.

Leave the brush from Eric's on your desk when you go to bed. Check in with me in the morning.

I am NOT going to steal from Eric! Think of another way to do whatever you have to do with the brush. I'm NOT stealing his.

That's why you bought the replacement brush. You're not stealing; you're just replacing something old with something new. I should also have mentioned that it's not Eric's brush, it's his father's, and it's one he hasn't used in months because he's started shaving his head. Even if you just took it he'd never notice it was gone.

This brush is very important to the plan, and it's very important that you get it tonight. Don't let anyone know you took it, don't be tempted to confess to Eric out of some misplaced feeling of guilt. Just go to his place, have a good time, and don't worry about it.

Trust me.

I got your stupid brush. It's clogged with dad hair—gross, and I had to touch it. Thanks a lot for that. If you want this thing, I'll put it in the desk's junk drawer and you can take care of it in a hundred years or whatever.

Eric's parents really weren't home and I stayed too late. By the time I realized it was after 9, it was dark out and Eric's got a provisional driver's license like mine and his parents don't let him drive after dark. He might have been able to get me home and get back before they returned, but they were supposed to be home by 10 and he wasn't supposed to go anywhere, so he couldn't risk it.

I don't have money for a cab (in part because certain people wouldn't let me so much as pick up a dollar if I found it lying on the ground because it might have "unforeseen consequences") and I couldn't take a bus because that same person who wants to keep me poor also has an anti-bus policy. It took me more than an hour to walk home, but it wasn't so bad because—creepy brush thing aside—going to Eric's and having some alone time with him was really nice. The walk gave me some time to think about it.

We really did homework for about half an hour. After that we talked and got kind of—let's say "snuggly." Now that I think about it, I'm not sure how much I walked on the way home because I was spending so much time floating. Having him so close and warm was more magical than anything you've shown me.

Sheesh—this really is sounding like a teen-girl diary. Sorry.

Still, if our relationship keeps going like this, maybe the journal really was worth all that gold. I'd never have met Eric without it.

I just added a rule to the beginning of the journal about not taking the bus. I don't remember why, but this has happened before. It's like I knew when I was writing it what the reason was, but forgot the second I was finished. There's no way to tell what would have happened if you'd taken the bus home, but whatever it was it was bad enough that I had to stop you from doing it. It's frustrating not knowing, but we both have bits of ignorance in our lives that we have to make ourselves content with, don't we?

I'm glad you walked and that it was a good walk. I'm glad that your evening with Eric was as good as I remember it being, and I understand your reluctance to mention the rather significant homework-to-smooching ratio in print, but I promise that nobody but you ever sees your writing in this journal. You shouldn't demean some rather glorious hand-holding and your first kiss (at least, the first one that counts) by calling it "getting snuggly."

You're right about Eric being worth a box of gold. More than that, really. He's probably the best thing that ever happens to you, and if you keep working with me, he'll be ours forever.

Leave the brush on your desk when you go to bed. Don't stick it in a drawer. Good night.

Sunday, March 17

It's a little after 2:30. I had a dream where I woke up because someone was in my room and I saw the silhouette of the man with one eye. He raised his hand slowly, pointing the palm at me, and I fell asleep. Then I woke up for real and I can't fall asleep again.

Taking the hairbrush is really bothering me. It's such a stupid little thing to worry about, but I still feel bad about taking it. I know it's just a hunk of plastic and that I replaced it with a new one, but there's something about a hairbrush that's so personal that it makes a difference. I've never even met Eric's dad but already I've taken something from him. The fact that it was old and disgusting doesn't make it any better. I'd still feel bad if I'd taken an old pair of used underwear and replaced it with a new one. Great— now, on top of everything else, I've grossed myself out with my own example.

I also feel bad about lying to Mom and Dad. I said I was going to study and there was, like you said, pretty much none of that going on. It was so good to feel Eric holding me and touching me that it makes me feel worse about lying. Getting something so nice in exchange for something so bad is like being a criminal.

Can you tell me it'll be all right?

I can tell you not to bother me with things like that. I've said before and I'll say again that this journal isn't a diary and I'm not an advice blog. The journal only has so many pages and once it's gone, it's gone. There's no getting another one. I like to hear you talk about Eric, but your angst is just a waste of paper.

Forget about Mom and Dad. Parents know that kids lie about what they do when they're together, Mom wouldn't object to you doing the "natural" thing, and Dad certainly doesn't have a problem with lying for recreational purposes.

Forget about the hairbrush, too. When you're tired or stressed, you worry about things you shouldn't worry about. You also say things you didn't intend to say. Don't think I don't notice.

Now GO TO BED

Dad was reading the news at breakfast and he said there was a shooting last night just two blocks from here. A man was driving when a car forced his truck onto the sidewalk, then two men dragged him into the street and shot him. The Times blog had a picture of the scene, and the truck the man was driving was the one that brought the package here. I'm sure of it.

Did I get him killed? Did someone kill him because they thought he had the gold, but he couldn't give it to them because I took it?

I remember hearing sirens when I was walking home, and I think I passed just a block from there at about the same time it was happening. If I'd taken the bus it would have gone down the street the man was shot on. Would the man in the truck have seen me in the bus window and pointed me out to the shooters? Or maybe a ricochet would have hit the bus if I'd taken it? Could that be why I had to walk?

On top of that, the hairbrush and razor blade are gone this morning. Did Melissa come for them? I don't want her in the house again—definitely not while I'm sleeping. Was I supposed to have woken up and fought off whoever came for the brush with the razor?

This is way too much for a Sunday morning. It's freaking me out.

You didn't get the man shot. He was a small-time criminal who blew something big and got other criminals mad at him. The police figure it out in a few days.

I don't know what would have happened if you'd taken the bus and we never will. You went right for the extremes with your speculation like you always do even when there are more likely mundane options. That's part of the curse of being a writer, but you need to recognize it in yourself and compensate. For example, if you'd been on the bus you probably would just have seen the crime scene before the police got it cleaned up and been so traumatized by the sight that you had trouble concentrating on the things we need to do. That would have been enough to derail our plans without jumping to you being hunted by criminals or shot.

I don't know for certain who took the brush and I don't know why the blade was taken or how they were taken. I have a suspicion but it doesn't matter. Forget about it. You need to get used to weird shit happening because it doesn't get any less weird from here on out and you have to keep your cool or we are completely screwed.

Get another razor blade out of the pharmacy bag and put it on the desk, right where the other one had been. After that, go take a bath, do some Facebook, ~~massage~~ message Eric, or whatever. After lunch, come back and I'll have something for you to do. It's nothing horrifying, dangerous, illegal, or scary, but it's not something you'll be thrilled about, so it would be better if you were relaxed.

Screw relaxing. What are you going to ask me to do?

Tear up the lottery ticket.

It was clever for you to wait until you saw that tomorrow's lottery has a big prize and no winner before you went back and wrote the winning numbers in the journal (although you won't do this now because it's in a timeline that got erased because you copied the numbers that I wrote). I know that to you it will look like the news says there was one winner, but I guarantee that when you originally wrote the numbers, the news reported there was none.

This isn't going to work. If you collect the lottery prize, Mom and Dad die. No kidding, no guessing, no tricks this time— they die. Being an orphan doesn't make you stronger. You're not Batman. If anything, you're a Cinderella who keeps throwing shit at her fairy godmother instead of just getting in the damned pumpkin.

It's ridiculous of you to even contemplate trying to keep a secret this big from me. I know you hid the ticket. Go find it. Destroy it.

I only kept it a secret because I knew you'd get all pissy about it. What if I never turn it in? Did you even think about that? Maybe I just want to see if it would win. Now that I know it did, I'll keep it hidden, like a memento that proves you're really there in the future. After a while, it will expire and you'll never have to worry about it again. It'll be our little bit of proof. I'll never show it to anyone. Hey, look! Nobody dies!

Liar. If you have it, you're going to try and collect on it. You can't fool me, and you shouldn't bother trying to fool yourself. You might really believe at this moment that you can let the thing expire, but pretty soon you'll talk yourself into cashing it. You know it. I know it. Get rid of it.

I'm trying to remember what I did with the stupid thing. I remember being frantic when I couldn't find it, and I remember being furious when someone claimed to have won, but I—now I remember: you gave it to Mom so that she could pretend it was hers when it won. How did you ever think that was going to stop me knowing that you were going against my infantilizingly clear instructions? Mom knowing about the ticket makes this much harder, particularly if she knows it's a winner. We shouldn't be involving her and need a way to back out of this.

You'll have to get another ticket. Make the numbers match the winning one so that Mom just thinks she misremembered the drawing date if she recalls what they were. That should be good enough. Replace the winning ticket with the new one and DESTROY the winning ticket. It's too dangerous.

If you collect the lottery prize, the family ends up all over the news. Some right-wing wacknado hears about it and gets it into his head to kill the "pagan foreigners" that "stole" the money he somehow thinks he deserved to win instead.

Save our parents! Get that ticket!

I'm an American. Mom and Dad aren't even immigrants.

This isn't an argument. Get a replacement. Burn the fucking ticket.

I can't. I don't know where it is because I don't know what Mom did with it after I gave it to her.

Okay, this is starting to weird me out. Maybe I should have listened. Tell me where it is and I'll do it.

I don't know where it is either. I remember Mom freaking out about winning when she checks the numbers tomorrow, but that pretty much overwhelms my memory for that day. Everything else is in the hole.

Well, maybe it's okay then. Maybe you can help me save them because you know what's going to happen. Maybe when we have the money, I can use it to help your plans?

Are you not listening to me? There's no saving Mom and Dad if that ticket is turned in. The money does help the plans move forward, but they move forward too quickly and with too much collateral damage. You keep talking as if I don't know what will happen if that ticket wins, but I do know because I'm living with the consequences.

I've done everything I can think of to stop you from buying it and letting it win, but it must be that there is no path forward other than the one we've taken so far. You have a day to find that ticket and replace it. Remember, don't just destroy it—replace it.

Monday, March 18

It's an hour until the lottery drawing and I've got cramping so hellbeast bad that I feel like I'm about to give birth to a refrigerator. I didn't even have lunch with Eric today. I told him I had to study in the library alone and my stomach was in such a knot that I didn't even buy lunch. We've been texting pretty constantly since Saturday and it's so hard for me to sound friendly and bubbly with him when I've got such a weight on me, but I can't tell him about any of this or he'll think I'm a freak, and if he clues in that I'm stressed he's going to think he did something wrong on Saturday, particularly if I refuse to talk about what's really wrong and I don't want to lie to him.

I didn't try to buy a replacement ticket on the way home because buying them is a pain and I was so sure I could work this out myself.

I didn't find the ticket. I looked everywhere I could think of. Mom's purse. Mom's car. The mail in-box. Where she thinks she can hide Christmas presents from me. The pockets of her laundry. Under things. Over things. In things. Everywhere. Every minute I've been home I've been sneaking around, looking for the damned thing and hoping Dad was too busy with pretending to work to notice how weird I'm being. Nothing.

I don't believe you that some crazy extremist is going to kill them if that ticket wins. If that really happened and I knew it was my fault, I'd go insane and kill myself. You're alive, so no matter what happens, even if it's something so bad that I end up wishing I hadn't won, it's not the murder thing.

Unless I'm completely wrong, in which case I'm completely, super, super, completely fucked. God, this is driving me INSANE!

I think I know a way out of this though. For it to work, we have to do an experiment.

I'm not allowed to look ahead in the book, but you're allowed to go back and change things you've already written. That's how you were able to add the rule about not taking the bus. Here's what I want you to do: After you've read this and are ready to respond, before you write anything, turn the page to see what I wrote and then begin your response to this message by writing what I will write in response to your message. Got that? If you do it, then your next message and my message after that will both begin with the same sentence.

This will be a great test of how well this book works because when I read the next page, if I don't like what you claim I'm going to write next, I can change it. If I change it, that will change what you wrote when you copied my writing and the cycle will start over. That should make a time feedback loop thing so we end up with the perfect thing written on the next page!

If that works, it could be a great way for us to make detailed plans without taking a lot of time because bad ideas will be written over by the time stream! We can consider something or refine an idea hundreds or even millions of times just by turning a page and leveraging our countless time-loop selves!

Now it's your turn: What's the next thing I'm going to write?

"I shouldn't waste pages with garbage like this."

At what point are you going to realize that no part of this is a game? If you want to do something useful that would change what's in this journal, then think good and hard about what I could have done to stop you from buying that ticket. Then, when you're in my position, do it.

I shouldn't waste pages with garbage like this.

You're right. I'm a complete screwup. I even just wrote what you said I was going to write because when the time came I was too scared of making a mess of things to dare try and change it.

You could have avoided causing a paradox by not turning the page and seeing what I wrote. I wonder if that's what you did. I could have found out by writing something different, but I feel paralyzed now when I even think of trying to do something on my own. You know everything and I don't know anything. Why did I even try to sneak around behind your back? My back?

Oh, God. Mom's yelling for me in the other room. I think she knows we won, but I thought the drawing wasn't for another 10 minutes. What am I supposed to do? They're going to expect me to be surprised and happy, but I can't do either. I just killed my parents, didn't I? I don't know what's going on. It's up to you. You have to find me a way out of this. What do I do?

Why didn't you respond? Is it because there's no way out?

There's no way out.

Welcome to one of the worst nights of your life.

Congratulations.

It's almost midnight. I want to die.

Mom thought she'd do something special with the lottery ticket since we almost never buy them. She brought it with her to Coven and "dedicated her will" to making it win. It was the biggest thing she'd ever tried to effect, and when there was the light show, she thought she'd succeeded. She didn't say anything to us about that part of the night so as not to get our hopes up.

Tonight, she was going to get the ticket and watch the web site for the numbers, but she couldn't find it. That's why she was yelling for me. When the numbers were drawn, she remembered them, saw we won, and got eyebugging insane.

After Coven, she put the ticket in a book for safekeeping. She couldn't remember what book she put it in, but when Dad was cleaning up the piles in the living room he took a bunch of "old junk" books to the library bookstore as donations. He said he didn't think he needed to ask her before getting rid of the books because they were his, and she turned it into a "so now we're not sharing things anymore?" argument and went on about how maybe they should split everything up right now and just get it over with.

I've never heard them argue like that. They were both yelling and both crying. I didn't have any idea what to do. I was sitting right there the whole time and they just kept going at it like I wasn't even in the room. Mom told Dad he has to go to the library in the morning and find the books, and he yelled "Fine!," stomped to his office, and slammed the door. I think I heard a picture fall off the wall.

Mom went to her room. I can still hear her crying.

If Dad finds the book, we're back to the murder scenario. If he doesn't find it, I don't even know what's going to happen. What do I do? Please?

He isn't going to find the book. I don't know how I didn't realize it back then, but I just figured out what happened to the ticket. It's not in the house and it's not at the library. You're never going to see it again.

I want to tell you what happened but I can't right now. I think it would be okay, but I'm not sure.

There's nothing you can do. The things you've put in motion are going to happen and you just have to let the train smash into the station. Go to bed. Tomorrow is going to be stressful and you need the rest.

I can't let this go. If you know where Mom put the ticket, then go back in the journal and tell me. I can find it and put it somewhere else before it's lost.

That wouldn't solve anything. After the ticket is purchased, all of the possible outcomes are bad. The only way out of this would be to stop you from buying the ticket in the first place, and obviously nothing I could have said would have stopped you from doing that. If you can think of something, do it when you're in my position. If not, then we have to suck it up and live with what we have.

Why don't you add not buying a lottery ticket to the stupid list of things I'm not supposed to do? Is that too obvious? Why won't you at least try to help me out of this!

Adding to the Don't list wouldn't help. All it would do is put the idea of buying a lottery ticket into your head earlier, and because you couldn't be convinced that buying a ticket is a bad thing you might end up thinking the whole Do/Don't list was something to question instead of something to obey. I can't risk that, particularly since I can't erase something I've written, only cross it out, and if "Don't buy a lottery ticket" was crossed out on the list, you'd practically take it as a command to buy one of the things and we'd never be able to find a way out of this.

You have to believe me when I say that I wish you hadn't bought that ticket even more than you do. I have tried absolutely everything I can think of to stop it from happening. You're asking why I won't help when I've been agonizing over a solution every night since it happened. You think I wouldn't do something if I could? You don't even have the smallest inkling of what I've been through. You don't know how hard it is to try and have a relationship with someone too pigskulled and stubborn to even trust herself. I wish you could see me. That would tell you all you need to know. For the love of God, you accuse me of not helping when if it wasn't for you and your arrogant fuckheadedness I'd still be

Stop. Stop. This gets us nowhere. My temper got us into this and we can't let it stop us from getting out. Remember that. No matter what happens, you need to stay calm. I'm not being a good example right now, but it's something we need to work on if we're going to squeeze some victory out of this spoiled fruit.

I don't even want to think about this anymore and you shouldn't either. We both need some rest. Please, go to bed.

Okay. I'm going to be calm and try to think this through. I think you're right about the bullet point thing, because everything you say rings true. But when you say that all possible outcomes after I buy the ticket are bad ones, are you really sure about that? Do you know for sure that if you tell me where Mom hid the ticket things go bad, or are you just assuming because you think that the timeline has written over a bunch of failed attempts? Well, there had to be a first time (for want of a better word) that you tried telling me about the hiding place, and maybe this is it. If it is and you try it and it fails then you do something different and the timeline gets rewritten. No big deal. You never even remember it.

Isn't that worth a try?

You almost had me convinced. I was seriously considering going back and telling you where the ticket was hidden, but now I can't.

When I turned to this page, there was a slip of paper between the pages warning me not to even contemplate sending you that information. This has never happened before and it terrifies me. We're too close to the edge. I don't want to die, not when we've come so far, not without seeing Eric again. Don't even ask me about this. I'm too afraid to talk about it. Please, please, please don't do anything like this again. There are forces at work that we are far too small to even contemplate fighting against. You will understand that in time. It will be revealed to you, and when it is, you will find one spark of hope in frozen blackness. I can't believe I came so close to turning that spark into a cinder.

We can't change what has happened. We have to move forward. Drop the subject.

Tuesday, May 19

I just saw the news on Twitter. I'm a murderer. You made me a murderer.

I have to leave for school but I don't know how I'm going to get through it. I killed a little girl. I should go to the police but they'd just think I was a nutjob or publicity troll.

How could you have done that? Do I become so callous that other people's lives mean nothing? What other horrible things have you had me do without my knowing? How can I stop you? Do I have to kill myself to keep me from becoming a monster?

I don't want any more of your lies. I'm not turning the page after I read this. I might never turn the page again. I don't want to be what I've become. Every time I see that little girl's smiling picture on the internet I want to die. She's on the cover of the paper. She's going to be staring at me every night when I close my eyes.

God damn you.

I know that learning about the hostage's death was traumatic, but you get over it. I also know that you turn the page and read this before leaving for school, even though you said you wouldn't, because it felt like the defiant thing to do. Sometimes, we don't make a lot of sense when we're mad.

You are in no way at fault for someone else committing murder. You are NOT responsible.

I can't remember how quickly the whole story comes out. I remember reading the article you saw the Twitter link to that talked about the hostage being executed because a promised ransom of gold was never received, but there's more to it than that.

You've obviously figured out that the letter you sent with our address in it arrived before the kidnapper's letter, causing the package to be delivered to you instead of to the next person in a chain of cutouts designed to stop the police from tracking the package. What you don't know is that the kidnappers never had any intention of returning the girl—I wish I could remember what her name was—to her parents. They knew that delivering the girl would be difficult without risking capture, and that an eight-year-old is more than old enough to be a witness that could have led to their capture.

Whether or not they received the ransom, they were going to do exactly what they did—leave her corpse in a ditch just off PCH. For all we know, by the time the gold was sent, she was already dead.

Calm down. Go to school. When you get home, write to me about what has happened. We will have things to discuss.

I thought this morning was the worst it could get. Even after what you wrote, I still feel like I killed someone. I couldn't breathe all day at school, like I was being wound tighter and tighter in cold, wet canvas that nobody else could see. I was afraid to come home because I might find the police waiting for me. Even worse, I might find a car full of criminal gunmen waiting for me at the curb, wanting to know where their money was, or holding Dad hostage because they found him at home.

It turns out I was afraid for the wrong reasons. I could hear Mom and Dad yelling even before I got to the front door. I don't know what Mom was doing home; maybe she didn't go to work at all. I don't know.

They were in the living room and I don't think they heard me come in. Mom was yelling about her coven. She was saying that Dad was jealous because he's always made light of it and now that they had the winning lottery numbers as proof of her magic abilities he couldn't deal with it.

Dad yelled back that he thought it was a load of crap. Mom said, "My mother—" and he cut her off with, "Was delusional!" I'd never heard him say anything like that before. I know he doesn't believe in magic, but he'd never said a word against Mom believing in it. He said that he knew exactly what went on at their Wednesday "meetings"—I could hear the quotes even in the yelling—

and it had nothing to do with Wicca and everything to do with perversion.

There was something about Mom accusing Dad of feeling threatened because she was showing she could take care of things herself, and something about Dad accusing Mom of being more interested in what she needed than what he did. I can't remember the details because they were yelling over each other. I did hear Dad say something about not having a choice about marrying her, and she shot back that he's never taken responsibility for his irresponsibility. I don't think I want to know what that means. He roared something like, "You're making no sense at all—I guess I should have realized that tits sag but crazy is forever!" It was too much.

I'd hurried down the hall at that point because things were way past my ability to deal. It's a good thing because Dad stormed out right after that and I don't want to know what he looks like when he's that mad. He yelled something about "going where the sane people are" and slammed the front door. It made me glad I hadn't interrupted them to try and explain that the whole problem wasn't him and Mom, but me and my secret magic book.

The quiet after that was as oppressive as the yelling had been. My head was screaming and I sat there on my bed feeling blackness press in on the edges of my vision.

I thought I was going to faint. Then Mom was standing there in the doorway. "I didn't know you were home," she said, her voice so tight that I could tell she was barely holding back tears. Her hands were shaking, just a little. She asked if I could get some money out of her purse and go out to get myself pizza for dinner. I think I nodded. Then she went into her room and closed the door. I could hear her sobbing, like her face was pressed into her pillow.

I texted Eric to see if he could meet me for pizza, but he can't. Now I'm worried that he's thinking something's wrong because I avoided him at lunch again. I'm ruining that too, aren't I? I'm turning everything to shit.

You were right about the lottery. You were right. You were right. You were right. I'm going to say that over and over until it's crawling into and under my skin like horrible, guilty, painful, unforgettable worms. You were right. Buying that ticket was the worst thing I possibly could have done.

The constant weight of anger and arguing makes them feel like strangers. I know there's been some tension about money, and Mom has made it abundantly clear that she thinks Dad is playing a few too many video games for someone who insists he's trying as hard as he can to find work. (I'd have to agree with that, actually.) Dad also hasn't upped the amount of stuff around the house he's doing very much even though he's working less, and that has been a sore point for a while. His giving away those books was more of his usual passive aggression against being asked to do something. But none of this had been more than prickly annoyances before.

Everything you said about them being murdered was bullshit, wasn't it? It was a ridiculous story, but you were trying to scare me away from buying a lottery ticket. I know now that if you'd told me that buying at ticket would lead to Mom and Dad going at each other with verbal assault rifles and Dad storming out, I never would have believed it. You had to lie. There really was nothing you could have written to stop me from stabbing my own future in the face.

Do you remember those nightmares about having a little brother who'd turn into a werewolf and threaten to claw me open whenever we were alone? We learned to wake ourselves up by having our dream self close her eyes and them open them as wide as she possibly could, which would make me open my eyes in real life. That was a perfect solution until the dream where when our eyes were closed Brother said, "That's not going to work this time," and when my dream self opened her eyes, he was flying at me with claws and teeth bared.

That's how I feel now. I'm desperately trying to open my eyes, but no matter how hard I try, reality keeps

being there. I'm trying to escape from a world that has
turned so completely around from the reality I know
that it literally must be a dream, but the harder I
try the more a voice keeps saying that opening my eyes
wider will only let me see more of the horror around me.

You really can stop worrying about the gold. The police never trace it to you and the kidnappers are killed when the police find them. All you did was write an address on a piece of paper. You didn't hurt anyone and you couldn't have helped anyone, either. It's just one more situation completely out of our control.

You're right about the threat of Mom and Dad's murder being bullshit. There's nothing else to say about that.

Even now, with the things you've just experienced well in my past, I can't think of anything to say that would have made me feel better after hearing that argument. At best, I could have told you to come home later so you missed it completely, but that would have put me in the position of having to explain why Dad was gone, and I don't think you would have believed me. Mom sure wouldn't have given you the whole story.

If there's anything I'm not thinking of that I can help you with, just ask. There is something you need to do tomorrow, but we don't have to talk about that now. Maybe after dinner.

What can I do to make them get together, calm down, and have a civil discussion about this? They're bringing in so many things to the issue that it's expanding out of control. Losing the ticket was a tragedy but it was an accident. We should all be being upset together instead of trying to point the finger.

I'm worried that if this doesn't calm down soon, they're going to both say too many things they can't take back and it will end up in divorce. Is that what's going to happen? Is preventing their divorce one of the things that you're trying to make better with all of this weirdness we're doing?

What did Dad mean about Mom's coven? I know they sometimes don't wear clothes, which is skeevie, but from the way he said it I think he thinks it's a big orgy or something. I know Mom wouldn't be involved in something like that, but tell me if there's something Dad knows that I don't.

Speaking of coven, should I tell Mom that it wasn't her spell to make the lottery ticket win that caused the light? Thinking that her magic worked really added to how mad she is at Dad. On the one hand, I don't like her being mad in part because of something that's a lie, but on the other hand it's hard to see how it would make her feel better to tell her that it was futureself me and not her behind the biggest work of magic she's ever done.

I don't think I can handle doing anything tomorrow. I don't know if I can even handle getting out of bed tomorrow.

One thing I can do is assure you that Mom and Dad don't get divorced. Pinky-cross doubletrue swear. There's nothing you can do about the arguing and nothing you can say to get them to be rational right now. Mom's going to be upset at everything; Dad's going to do the stupid shit he's going to do.

I should warn you that this isn't as bad as it gets. There are worse things than arguing. There are going to be times when you feel like you're drowning in the whitewater stress of it all, but you need to remember that I'm proof that you live through it and past it. There's air up there if you can just force yourself to keep swimming toward the surface.

Forget what Dad said about Coven. He was just saying the thing that he knew would bother Mom most. Dad morphs into a major asshole when he's mad. Remember the Fourth of July right after Dad lost the golf tournament account when he got so mad about a dumb joke that he threw Uncle Matt's man purse into the pool? Or when he woke you up walking down the hall in the dark, you heard him trip on something, and the next day you found Orange Bear in the trash out back? We're lucky we have only seen it a couple of times, but the guy loses his head when he loses his shit.

You understand now that Mom's Coven really can do magic if they're given the chance. It isn't their fault that the traditions and ceremonies they're following were watered into worklessness by misguided romantic fiddling and tendencies toward sympathetic magic instead of scientific inquiry. When they called that light, they were able to draw the plane of separation a little nearer. That's going to help bring a power across from the other side that will bring us closer to our goal. None of that would have been possible without your help.

Forget about trying to explain about switching the magic ingredients to Mom. You're right that it won't help anything and you'd be putting yourself in a weird position where you're practically begging her to ask questions that you don't want to—and can't—answer.

Let's talk about tomorrow. You won't want to hear this, but tomorrow is too important for you to sit out. If you do, you will literally, no bullshit, be dead within a month. I can't tell you more than that because—for very complicated reasons— if I tell you about it, it will make it more likely that you will die.

On your way home from school tomorrow, you need to go back to the Black Heart. There is something Melissa wants you to do and I promised her that you would as part of her payment for helping us. She doesn't want me to say any more about what she needs—I think she kind of likes leaving people uncomfortable—but this is big enough that we need to just go with it. We need this. Believe it or not, Melissa is going to make everything better.

One last thing, you need to see Eric at lunch tomorrow. Tell him you're upset because things are bad at home. He won't push for details and being with him will help ground you for what's coming.

Wednesday, May 20

I'm glad Melissa didn't let you try and prepare me for this because there's no way you could have. The woman is a complete, fuckshit crazy freak. I would love never to have anything to do with her again and it doesn't thrill me that I'm apparently going to be best buds with her at some point in my future. I hope to God that you're only working with her because of what you need her to do for you, because if you actually like her I'm going to take that as a sign that I'll be coming down with a serious case of brain damage at some point.

When I went into the Black Heart, Melissa was arranging some things on that table near the rear wall. She looked up when I came in the door and just stood there looking at me expectantly. I didn't know what else to do so I walked back to where she was and said, "I was asked to come here and help you with something."

"Of course," she said, like that was a normal thing to say. She pulled a black-and-red hand-carved chair back from the table and gestured for me to have a seat.

I sat.

On the table in front of me was a pair of glass vials with cork stoppers, a pair of scissors, several long bone needles, a black stone box, and a set of three daggers, each of a different metal. It was like a scene from

a spy movie where the villain shows the hero a tray
of nasty-looking medical equipment to intimidate him
into talking, only in this case the villain is from the 19th
century, massively eccentric, and incapable of buttoning
a blouse all the way up.

"What do you want me to do?" I asked. My palms were
actually sweating, which was something I thought only
happened in novels.

"Just sit there," she said. "Answer a couple of questions.
It won't take long."

Then she walked around the chair so she was standing
behind me and put her hands lightly on my shoulders.
Her touch managed to feel both light and oppressive,
like my shoulders were being brushed with the delicately
carved fingers of a marble statue. She slid her fingers
slowly from my shoulders to my neck and back, tracing
the bone. It made the hair on my neck stand up and
for a second I thought I had stumbled into a two-girl
slumber party scene so ridiculous that I could practically
smell the very, very lonely guy who wrote it.

"Thank you for the gold," she said. "I couldn't have made
use of the book without it, and that helps us both, doesn't
it?" It wasn't really a question, so I didn't answer.

"I'm a very rich woman now," she continued. "Wealth
doesn't mean much in and of itself, but it makes many

things so much easier. I want you to think of what you want most right now. It could be money, it could be love, it could be security—anything. Do you have something in mind?"

I did. You know what I was thinking of. I somehow knew that she did, too. I nodded.

"Good," she said. "If you could have what you're thinking of right now, would you take it if the price was the death of someone close to you?"

"No!" I blurted. I tried to stand, but the statue hands were unmoving; a reminder of her holding that box of gold like it was a box of tissues.

Melissa laughed a little. It was a pretty laugh, which was sort of disconcerting in and of itself. "I didn't think so," she said, "but I had to ask. Did you know that there are plenty of people who would accept a bargain like that? Not nameless strangers, but people you've met who would buy love, for example, with the death of someone to be named at a later date. It's a ridiculous bargain and the people who make it deserve what they get. I'm glad you're smart enough to see that."

Her hands lifted and she went around me to the table, picking up the vials and scissors. "This is all we'll need, then," she said, looking down at me and smiling thinly.

"What are you going to do?" I asked, turning to follow her as she walked around the chair again. I really didn't like her going behind me with that stuff, but how could I protest when I'd gotten myself into this? You can't buy a ticket to a haunted maze and then complain when they say it's your turn to go in.

"Keep facing forward," she said. "What I'm about to do will be unpleasant for a moment, but what it's going to do is save your life. It's the least I can do for all you're doing for me." I felt her lift a few strands of my hair, followed by a hint of a tug and the click of the scissors.

I started to protest, but she cut me off. "I don't have to do this, you know. I could take what I need and let you die or live in misery. Count your blessings."

She put the scissors and one vial on the table. The vial was stoppered and held a lock of hair, but the hair was white—not like mine at all.

Melissa walked behind me again. "This next part is going to hurt," she said. "It will be brief, but you need to sit perfectly still and not make a noise."

Don't think of the white bear. Easy.

I felt her palms come to rest on the sides of my head, fingertips on my cheeks. "Don't move," she said. There was a touch of air in my hair, and I got the impression

that she was saying something soundlessly. Then I felt
a wrenching, screaming pain, like a healthy tooth was
being yanked from my head by a brute with pliers. In
that instant, I noticed that in the display case across
the room from me I could see a reflection of Melissa
standing behind me with eyes closed and an empty
expression on her face, her hands at her sides even as I
could feel her fingers digging into my cheeks.

The pain was over in an instant and I cried out—okay,
screamed—instructions to the contrary be damned.
I could taste a rush of blood in my mouth. I jumped
up from the chair and fell back from Melissa, my back
slamming into the wall, my hands searching my face
for the hole she'd clawed. "You pulled my fucking tooth!"
I yelled.

Melissa placed the second vial on the table next to the
first. It held a molar, bloody with pulp. "I did no such
thing," she said.

The damndest thing was, she was telling the truth.
I could taste the blood, I could feel the pain, but no
matter how my tongue searched it couldn't find an
empty space anywhere. My teeth were all intact. My
hands found no evidence of the mangling surgery.

After a moment of uncomfortable silence, Melissa
began to gather the things from the table, as if she had

lost interest in me. "You can go now," she said. "We're done. Sorry about the pain."

I wanted to say something, but had no idea what. That's when I noticed that the door to the store's back room, only about ten feet away, was open and that someone was standing in it. It took me a second to recognize Olivia, dressed even more gothic than usual if that's possible, glaring like there weren't enough daggers in the world for all the stabbing she wanted to do to me.

I still didn't know what to say, but the moment I opened my mouth to see if something sensible would come out, Melissa said, "Go," without even looking up.

So I did.

Now's the point where you come clean and tell me everything—EVERYTHING—that's going on here. You're constantly evading and telling me it's for my own good and that I have to trust you, but you know better than anyone that the longer I hear that the more bullshitty it's going to smell.

The whole thing with the hair and the tooth—that was the weirdest, most deeply disturbing experience of my entire life. I can't go through something like that again. I can't even imagine being able to sleep again without that vial of gore floating before me every time I close my eyes. What was that REALLY for? What did Melissa mean when she said she was saving my life? I need more than just promises that all is going to be well if you want anything more than random cussing and fuckyous going forward.

What is the point of all this? Why are we doing this? Why am I doing this? I thought you said you were going to take care of Mom and Dad, but their relationship is closer to ground zero than I ever imagined it could be. I'm doing things with magic forces that I didn't even believe in before this started and going on errands that feel as innocuous as putting on a ring until I find out the ring was pulled from a hand grenade that I suspect was shoved in my mouth by a freaky phantom dentist.

No more vague. I need answers.

You aren't going to get everything you want. I'll do the best I can.

A lot of what we're doing is prompting things that were going to happen anyway to happen faster than they would have otherwise. You know in your heart that Mom and Dad were on the skids long before this. They were keeping their problems bottled up, but they were there. How long has it been since you took a family vacation, even for a weekend? When was the last time you saw them just sitting in the same room quietly reading together? Have you ever wondered how they got together in the first place when they seem to have so little in common? Your buying the lottery ticket brought things to a head, but it was going to happen eventually anyway.

What Melissa did—I can't exactly explain it, but she'd say that she bound your life force to your body. The hair is because she needs hair to have an influence on someone's body. I have to wait to tell you what the business with the tooth was, but it's a good thing that can save you if you get yourself in a really bad spot. If you follow instructions, you'll never need it.

The reason she did all this is that things are about to get very dangerous, not just for you, but for the world. If you listen to me, trust me, and follow my instructions, you'll avoid anything else traumatically disturbing and will never be in any real danger. If you don't, you'll see things that you'd spill blood to misremember and do things that would have ended your life without Melissa's influence.

There are bigger horrors than a tooth in a jar that I still see every night. I need your help stopping those things from happening, and if I tell you what they will be, then your imagining and obsessing over them will be almost as bad as if they actually happen. I couldn't take that.

I'm frightened of Melissa more deeply than I've ever been frightened of anything. At the same time I am thoroughly in awe of what she can do and how masterfully she works her will, like she's weaving a beautiful cloak from the world around her. I would love to never have to deal with her again, but I ache with worry that she will never return if I don't do what needs doing. I hate having to rely on my younger self because everything I put you through, I put myself through. But it has to be done. Without you and Melissa, I can never leave this house again. Without you and Melissa, I will never see Eric again.

As much as you are attracted to Eric now, it only becomes stronger. I don't think he's in any danger, but I can't go to him and I'm not even sure he knows I'm still alive. Every moment of separation is a sharp-beaked thing tearing its way out of my heart. You and Melissa are the only hope I have of getting him back and raising a palace out of this cesspool.

If you quit now, you'll end up trapped, alone, hopeless, and wishing for death.

Every detail of this is important, but it's all I can say. Please, please be patient.

I don't have time to be patient! Everything is going to hell and, just to give you something YOU don't want to hear for a change, I think YOU'RE part of the problem!

We're both under a lot of stress but I think all those bad experiences have made you too cautious. You're trying to fix every little detail, but I think what we need to do is kick this shit in the ass and go an entirely new way.

You keep harping about my making bad decisions, but maybe we can take one of those decisions and turn it to an advantage. You didn't want me to buy the lottery ticket because you knew it would lead to trouble for Mom and Dad. Okay, I get that. It was a mistake, but it's a done deal so we should make the best of it.

You said you figured out what happened to the ticket but are afraid of a little note—from Melissa, right?—telling you to keep it secret. Well, fuck her! Let's turn all our efforts to getting the ticket back. The prize is literally hundreds of millions of dollars, and I bet that if we had that kind of money a whole lot of options would be open that we hadn't even considered before. We could buy Melissa's shop right out from under her and then who would be in the catbird seat?

Maybe you're worried that someone else already has the ticket and won't give it to us. I've got an answer for that.

When I went to buy the ticket, the guy at ShopStop asked for ID when I gave him the order form with the numbers on it. I got denied because I'm underage and playing dumb didn't get me anywhere. I was going to go home and try to convince Mom to buy the ticket, even though she doesn't—or didn't—believe in gambling, but I got stopped by a man who was waiting on the sidewalk.

This was the strangest man I've ever almost literally run into. He was white, tall, and wearing a tight T-shirt that showed he was all wiry muscle. The weirdest thing was that he had a missing eye—no eye patch or anything, just this gaping hole in his face. It should have been horrifying.

He was just standing there and I was paying so little attention to the world around me that I came close to slamming right into him. Instead, he grabbed my shoulder with one hand, firm enough to stop me but not hard enough to hurt. I was still carrying the order blank and my $20, and he held out his other hand, gesturing toward them. I thought I was being mugged, but he was so calm and matter-of-fact that it caught me off guard. Some people with disabilities or a striking appearance give off a "you look at me too long or say the wrong thing and there's going to be an ass-kicking" vibe, but this guy was broadcasting something more like

"I'm not worried about it so why should you be?" Before I knew what I was doing, I'd handed over the cash and order form.

The guy never said a word, but made a "just a second" gesture and walked into the ShopStop. When he walked in, a guy in a baseball cap looked up at him and reflexively jumped back, right into a rack of cookies that he sent spraying across the floor. The woman behind the counter saw One Eye but didn't say anything, and a woman who was about to buy a soda gestured to let him go first. He bought the ticket with no trouble and was back out the door while baseball-cap was still picking up cookies.

When he got back to me, One Eye handed me my order blank and ticket and just walked away. If he had any expression at all, it was from the Mona Lisa school of emoting. I never even thought to thank him.

Here's the point of my going over all of this: That guy is our witness. He's proof that the ticket is mine, so if someone already has it, he can prove it isn't theirs. I don't know who the man is, but he walks around with a missing eyeball, so how hard could it be to find him, particularly with you having time and living in the future? Once we locate him, we offer him a million dollars to help us out and we're good to go. Doesn't that sound better than keeping secrets, weird bullshit, and relying on the dubious promised fruits of painfucking ghost dentistry?

If it all goes to hell or doesn't work out, you just go back in the diary, write "It didn't work out" on the page after this one, and we look for something else to do.

It won't work out. We don't even have to try.

Security footage at the ShopStop would show that it wasn't you who bought the ticket, and even if it didn't, someone buying the ticket for you is still illegal because you're underage. They wouldn't give you the money and they might even rule the ticket invalid and give it to nobody. Come to think of it, my original idea for having you buy a replacement ticket wouldn't have worked for all these same reasons— you're too young to buy a ticket.

All of that's irrelevant, though.

The man who bought the ticket for us is named Kurt. He's Melissa's partner. They had the ticket, but it's gone now. I don't know the whole story, but if I understand it correctly Melissa made an arrangement with some kind of financial broker so that as soon as the winning numbers were announced he'd buy the ticket from her immediately for something like 80% of its value. She lost tens of millions of dollars on paper, but it got her the money immediately instead of having to wait for the government to process payment and it kept her completely out of the news.

With the way things are about to go, the state will never pay out the prize anyway.

No matter what you do, don't get it into your head that you can outmaneuver Melissa. It isn't going to happen, and all you can get for trying to slap out fire is burned.

The bitch! If she's going to steal our money, she should at least give us half. If the world's getting so messed up so soon, what is she going to do with it anyway?

And why didn't the journal stop this from happening? I thought that if something truly devastating happened, we'd get some kind of feedback loop that wouldn't let the future go forward unless it was fixed? That money was our ticket out; doesn't this count as devastating?

Melissa considers the lottery ticket to be part of our payment for helping us use the journal, so she doesn't feel like she owes us anything. It may not seem fair, but you have to admit that it's hard to put a price on something that gives you the ability to change the past—or at least try to. The fact that we aren't doing as well with it as we might hope doesn't enter into it. At least, not from her perspective, and I'm not inclined to try and argue the point with her.

The journal can't stop every possible bad thing from happening. If the problem isn't big enough to stop you from going forward, then it doesn't matter to the journal. It's kind of like evolution—if something doesn't stop an animal from reproducing, evolution doesn't care. Evolution can't stop cancer because most people who die from cancer are already done having all the children they are going to have.

You want to know what Melissa is going to do with all that money? You're right that there is a lot of power in wealth like that. Melissa is using it to buy people and things she needs to call the Patrons to reform the earth. It would be difficult for me to explain exactly what that means, and you're going to know soon enough anyway. The important point is that she was going to do this with or without the money; the money just lets her be more efficient.

I take it that the future you live in is one where Melissa's plan has succeeded or is about to succeed. Is that why you're separated from Eric? Are all these things we're doing leading up to disrupting her plan so we can be with him?

We don't want to disrupt her plan; we want to help her accomplish it faster. That sounds insane, but let me explain.

If the Patrons come into the world slowly, society falls apart. Countries try to insulate themselves from the problem, stop trusting their neighbors, and begin blaming each other. Religious groups form and throw accusations at easy targets, leading to riots and horrible public executions. Wars arise over resources and imagined threats. Humanity is so weakened by all of this that the Patrons destroy everyone. I get the feeling that I wrote that as part of another version of the journal, from a future where we weren't able to make a difference, so I'm confident that is what would happen without our help.

On the other hand, if Melissa can pull the Patrons across quickly, all over the globe, humanity comes together to fight a global threat. It's still devastating and world-changing, but not completely apocalyptic. There's a chance for people to survive, and maybe even form one world culture where old political and prejudicial boundaries don't have the strength they once did. That's what we're fighting for.

I guess that technically, if we are looking at this as cold equations, the lottery money works in our favor. It certainly helps Melissa work faster. The reason I wanted to avoid it was completely personal: It still hurts to think of Mom and Dad arguing like that, and I wanted there to be more family time before things got to the point they are at now. I could have used their support when I was sitting where you sit.

Mom and Dad are going to be okay. I know it in my heart. You said yourself that they don't get divorced, so this is something we can get over. Is it weird that your being depressed about this is actually making me feel more confident about it?

Does it strike you as odd that we're fighting Melissa by helping her? Is there any chance that she can't succeed without us? Was the plan to do this with the journal yours or hers? Do you remember talking to her about it? Is there some leverage you haven't considered using, maybe?

I have instructions from Melissa detailing certain things to do with the journal—like getting the hairbrush. Other things were, I assume, my idea, although it's possible that they are ideas given to me by Melissa in a timeline that no longer takes place. Either way, I don't remember talking to Melissa about the plan to move things forward quickly. There are a lot of things I've forgotten, though.

I'm confident that there is no leverage that can be used against Melissa, and even if there were I'd have to give it a second, third, fourth... hundredth thought before trying to use it. There is no path to success that involves going against her. I've seen others try.

I owe Melissa my life. She's shown me a lot of truth I'd have been completely ignorant of otherwise, and if it weren't for her I'd be dead because of my own stupidity and temper.

Sometimes hope has the devil's face. Keep that in mind. Always.

You're too afraid to even look for something that could be used to your advantage and I'm the stupid one? If you're old enough that you're losing your memory, then how are you sure that you're thinking clearly enough to be doing any of this? Maybe you should let me do more. Trust your younger self who doesn't have so much emotional baggage. With you in charge, things have gotten pretty fucked up. I'd say that's a sign that we need new leadership.

I'm not old; I have a head injury. That's where my "memory hole" came from. I lost some memory and some fine motor control, and I have to deal with constant pain, but other than that there's no problem with my thinking. If you do as I say, I won't be injured and won't have this handicap to deal with, so even that won't be an issue any longer.

Forget about trying to convince me that you should be the one making decisions. It's your stupidity and temper that got me here, injured, trapped, alone, unable to contact Eric. I'm in a perfect place to know exactly how bad things get because of you, so I'm not exactly giddy over the idea of you doing more on your own when you're the one who crippled me.

And no, I won't tell you how you get injured. It's for all the usual reasons. All I'll say is that you need to keep that razor on the desk and remember that when the time comes and I say to use it, you cannot hesitate, not even for a moment.

Well, fuck. I was starting to feel a little better until you reminded me that I am running low on emotional support and will soon be needing to defend myself with a razor to avoid having my head bashed in. Letting me Know that the person I'm supposed to rely on is a brain-damaged version of myself doesn't help matters either.

I need something more than that to hold on to. I'm pretty sure Eric is falling in love with me, and I know I'm in love with him. You telling me that we end up being in love so strongly that he's more important than the world to me just makes that a fatal accompli.

You're all about getting things to move more quickly, so how about this: Eric invited me over to study again tomorrow, and I don't think his parents are going to be home until late. I'm going to go all the way with him. I Know he wants to, I know I want to, and you wouldn't tell me when I'm going to lose my virginity, so I'm telling you. After tomorrow night, Eric is going to be so in love with me that there will be no separating us, no matter what comes. I don't know if that will stop you from being unable to leave the house, but I bet that it will make sure that Eric is there with you.

I'm taking the lead on this one. Unless you're going to tell me to use a condom, grandma, there's nothing for you to say on the subject. We can pick up with your "ruin the future faster" plan after that.

That is such a pathetic cry for help. Eric knows you're under stress and he's too perfect a guy to do something that would feel like taking advantage of the situation, even if he thought you were ready to go there in your relationship, which he doesn't. You're thinking right now that you can seduce him anyway, but even if you try that you're just going to make him lose respect for you. This is all about your desperation for someone to turn to and your wanting to lash out at me. It's an ignorant, juvenile fantasy and it's going to get you nowhere.

I can't tell you what to do, but I CAN tell you what you did. You don't have sex with Eric tomorrow and, if you don't listen to me, you're not going to have sex with him ever.

You need to get in line. You need to stop fighting and cooperate. You need to respect my position and my knowledge and for once in your life just trust. You can't be at Eric's house tomorrow night. You got that?

No.

Thursday, May 21

Fuck you.

I walked to Eric's with him after school. His parents were supposed to be going to some dinner thing straight after work and not be home until after ten. Instead, his mom came home when we'd only been there less than an hour and walked in on us in the living room while I was still trying to get us past kissing. She completely flipped out, threw me out, and said she never wanted to see me again. She was on the edge of crying and I thought she was massively overreacting because she's hyperprotective or something. It turns out, not so much.

A little later, Eric texted me. Part of what his mom was freaked out about was that he'd turned his cell phone off when we got to his place and she'd been trying to get a hold of him. There had been an explosion at this high-energy research place where Eric's dad works, and his dad was injured. Eric's mom wanted Eric to meet her at the hospital, but she had to come home for him when he didn't answer his phone. The explosion was a big deal. It's all over the internet.

Things aren't much better here. Dad didn't come home for dinner; Mom just ordered delivery and cried in the living room while I sat at the table and tried to make myself eat.

I saw on Facebook that after school there was also a fire at Olivia's house. She was able to get out but her sisters both died. I don't even like her, but seeing her at the Black Heart makes me think there is some kind of connection to this whole business. If I was to dig deep enough, I'd find that I was responsible for the fire and for their dying, wouldn't I? Just like I'm responsible for Mom and Dad. Just like my taking that hairbrush was probably the chaos butterfly that got Eric's dad caught in an explosion.

I'm not being paranoid. I've been watching for news about that girl whose ransom gold we took. The police now say that she was alive until soon before they found her, which means that the kidnappers didn't kill her until after they didn't get their ransom. The police found the house where it happened and say she was drowned in a bathtub. I'm smearing bullshit on your saying I'm not responsible. I feel like my hands were around her throat and pushing her under water, burning down a house, blowing up a lab, tearing apart a family.

My life wasn't great before this journal, but it wasn't a disaster and it didn't strike out at everyone around me.

You're manipulating me—I'M manipulating me, if that even makes sense—and the more I think about your explanations the less sense they make.

There's a solution to this you haven't considered: I burn the journal. I set fire to it right now. You never get it, I never hear from you, none of this happens. Maybe Melissa's little plot goes forward slower than you would like, maybe the world suffers, but if it does, it's not because of me. I can find another way to get together with Eric. It's a win for everybody—at least, everybody I care about.

Give me one good reason not to stick this piece of shit in the oven.

Do we really have to keep doing this? If you insist on internalizing everything and trying to make it about you, I'm going to end up spending all my time talking you down from a tree you should never have climbed in the first place.

Nothing is nearly as bad as you think it is.

- Eric's dad is going to be fine. He messed up a setting on some kind of experimental machine that caused it to overload and explode, but he wasn't even in the room when it happened. He's going to have some scars, but that's it.

- Eric is going to get grounded and that IS on you. I told you not to go over there.

- When your former crush Colin sees that Olivia is distraught about the tragedy in her family, he ends up trying to make her feel better and they start dating. The last I heard they were a happy couple—or, at least, as happy as anyone is.

- Yes, the kidnappers killed the girl after the ransom went missing, but they were going to kill her anyway. When they killed her, they still thought the ransom was coming and were "cleaning up loose ends" so they could take off as soon as they had their gold.

Everything else I've explained before and I'm not going to do it again. Nothing's stopping you from going back and rereading.

You could say that some of the things that happened wouldn't have happened without you, but that's true of the consequences of every breath you take. This isn't a Christmas movie where if you disappeared from the picture everything would suddenly be a unicorn tea party. If we weren't doing anything, the world's fuse would still be burning, just more slowly and with more certain destruction at the end.

Every time you mess up, blame yourself, disregard directions, or fly off the handle you're making it harder for me to believe that I'll ever leave this house or get Eric back. All of that is the consequence of who I was and who you are. You threatening to burn the one thing that gives us hope makes me think that maybe I deserve what I've got, not because of anything I did, but because of what a worthless, self-centered waste of time I was.

Do you remember when we were eight and cut off Happy Dog's head because we wanted to see if Mom was lying when she said stuffed animals didn't have guts? He was never the same because even when his head got sewn back on the stitches made him look like a monster instead of a friend. Part of you still hates eight-year-old you for doing something that stupid. What if you could go back and tell your past self that if she cut off Happy Dog's head she'd be miserable, but even though she knew you were from the future, she went to the kitchen and got the knife from the cutting block anyway? Wouldn't you want to slap her, yell at her, and tell her that she needed to listen?

That's how I feel about you. Just drop the knife and put Happy Dog down. Maybe you'll never get the answer to your stupid question about stuffed-animal guts, but you'll have years more of a good friend to hold when you sleep.

By the way, the journal's fireproof.

Fine. It sounds like, for all your hard work, I never do grow out of being a self-important know-it-all bitchling.

Even if I take all your explanations at face value and not as more lies to manipulating me into following your secret plan, we still agree that buying the lottery ticket was my screwup, right? That means the consequences of that are at least partly my fault, despite your word-game philosophy shenanigans, and those consequences sure as shit seem to be a double-time death march toward divorce, all unreliable reassurances to the contrary aside.

Dad hasn't been home since last night. I tried calling him but he didn't pick up. He always turns his ringer off when he's not expecting a call, so that was no big surprise, but it's still frustrating. That ticket caused the argument that made him leave. I want you to tell me where he is so I know he's not off getting murdered as part of your master plan.

You don't want to know where Dad is. If I tell you, you'll try to find him no matter what I say, and doing that leads to something much worse, including one of those memories that I don't want to have in my head.

He's fine, he's not in danger, but you MUST NOT try and see him. Mom and Dad are adults. You need to let them work through things on their own and not try to interfere.

Besides, we're getting near to the end of all of this and things are about to become critical. I need your head clear and free from distractions. There's nothing more to do for a few days. Take a break. You won't be able to text Eric for a couple of days because his mom took his phone away as part of being grounded, but you can see him at school. Concentrate on your relationship; have lunch with him tomorrow; build some nice memories.

There's no school Monday. At noon, Google "car dealership exploding man" and watch the video that comes up. Let me know what you see and we'll go from there.

I tried to think of what it could be that has you all traumatized about the possibility of my hunting down Dad. He's not dead or badly injured or you would have said something about getting him help or him being beyond help. I thought about the worst thing I could find if I located him, and that was him beaten up or passed out vomitface drunk somewhere. That would definitely be a sight I'd want to forget, but with all I've been through already, I couldn't imagine being traumatized for life by something like that, even though it was after dark.

Chock-full of not giving a damn about what you think and doubting completely that you ever tell the whole truth, I went over and over all possible Dad-related horrors in my mind, figuring that mental desensitizing would help me if there really was something to worry about. If it was bad, then all that depression exercise would help me get over it; if it was something less than mindwrecking, I'd be relieved.

I used the app on my phone to locate Dad's phone so I'd know where he was. I thought he'd be in a restaurant or a hotel, or just sitting in his car or a park somewhere, but instead he was in a house at an address I didn't recognize less than two blocks from here. That didn't make any sense.

Mom was in her room with the door closed so I just left and walked down there. I wasn't exactly in a mood to take you at your fatalistic word and thought that maybe I could talk Dad into coming home and we could all work things out.

It was a little blue house with a desert-landscape front yard. All the lights except the porch light were out, so I checked the app again to confirm that's where he was. It said he was inside, only a few feet away. I walked up to the front door and just stood there for a second, listening. I didn't hear anything, not even a TV. I was going to knock, but I knew this had to be the moment where the thing you didn't want to remember would happen. Maybe this was where my knock would make the door slowly open to reveal him passed-out drunk, or maybe I was wrong about him not being hurt and he was lying on the floor, the dismembered victim of some psychopath. Maybe this was just the house of a career criminal who'd mugged him and stolen his phone.

I was thinking that instead of knocking, maybe I should go around the house and see if I could hear conversation or see a light in the back. While I was trying to get over being frozen with indecision, I heard a cat. The harsh, bare porch light made weird shapes where it broke up the dark, so it took me a second to see a brown cat with a white ear walking out of the shadow of a big cactus in the yard. It was the same cat that had followed me home the other day when I had the can of tuna.

It was Amy's cat; this was Amy's house. Dad was at Amy's house, inside, with the lights out.

I almost pounded on the door, but you stopped me. I suddenly knew what I was going to find if I went in there, and I didn't want that. Not at all. What was I going to do anyway? Chastise Dad for having an affair? Shame him into coming home? Even I'm not clueless enough to think that would do anything but make it worse.

I ran home but managed not to start really sobbing until I got back to my room.

I need you tell me what it was you stopped me from seeing. Then I need to you tell me how my finding a cat that let Dad meet the woman he was going to have an affair with doesn't make me responsible for it. I've been mad and demanding before with my questions, but this time I really need it. I need to know how this could possibly be for the better. I can't think of any way, and I can't handle the thought that I might be the one who crafted the nail that was the last in their marriage's coffin.

For a minute, I thought that standing on the doorstep and realizing that Dad was having an affair was the memory I wanted to escape, but it wasn't. I can't think of anything from that incident that I'm not over. I think your hesitating long enough to see the cat and then leaving was enough to prevent whatever it was from happening. Maybe I knocked and found the door unlatched, or maybe I went around back when nobody answered, and either way caught them together. Probably something like that, but it didn't happen, so I don't remember.

You blew it by tracking Dad down, but in the end you did the right thing and that saved us from a nightmare, if not from a larger repercussion that we'll talk about later. I don't know why I was so anxious about you not going after Dad when you ended up not being traumatized by it. Maybe it's because if I'm not anxious you end up being traumatized? I hate the paradox of all of this as much as you do. I hate not feeling in control.

Getting you to bring the cat home is one of the few specific things in the instructions Melissa left. She must have known I would have asked you to do something to stop Dad from meeting Amy, so she gave me a brief explanation of why it needed to happen.

If Dad didn't meet Amy, then he would have stayed home even though he and Mom were arguing all the time. Because of that, he'd be home when a Patron arrives and you would see him literally ripped to pieces in front of your eyes. You'd be horribly injured, too, but wouldn't die because of what Melissa did—you'd just live for years in horrible, mutilated pain.

Now, though, Dad won't be home, which means that the Patrons won't come in the house. You won't have that horrible memory and they won't hurt you.

I don't want to talk anymore about that because I'm worried about accidentally saying something that will mess things up. I'll just say that, as awful as Dad having an affair is, it's definitely the lesser evil compared with seeing him murdered. If there's another way this could have been handled that would have worked out, I don't know what it would be.

Try to put it out of your mind as best you can. Write Monday after you watch the video.

5/22

The police are here! What do I do???

Crap—I forgot about that.

Answer the door. Say your parents aren't home. They just leave a card.

No big deal.

OMG, I thought I was going to stroke out. I looked out the window because I heard car doors close and I saw two men in suits coming up the walk. I saw the badge on one of their belts and thought they were coming for me.

I thought you said that the package of gold wasn't going to be traced to me? That has to be what they're looking for. What if they noticed how nervous I was? What am I supposed to do when Mom calls them? How am I supposed to explain to Mom why the police were here?

And most importantly, why didn't you warn me about this???

I didn't warn you because it was such a bunch of nothing that it didn't even stick in my mind. I said the package wouldn't be traced to you and it hasn't been. The police are grasping at straws. If they notice you're nervous, they'll assume it's because you're home alone and the police just showed up for no reason. They don't suspect you of anything and probably just want to ask if anyone saw that truck in the neighborhood on the day the gold went missing. That's fine because nobody did.

Tear up the card and flush it. Don't bother telling Mom. The police never come back.

You need to start concentrating on keeping a cool head. All you need to do to get through situations like this is not freak out.

I was doing a good job of keeping my freaklevel low until the police showed up.

Eric is seriously grounded. He's not supposed to even talk to me for a week, but we had lunch together anyway. It's hard to know exactly what happened because Eric is a bit shaky on the details, but it sounds like his dad somehow managed to remove some shielding from around a high-energy particle experiment that was in progress and the whole machine "lost containment" and exploded. His dad has cuts and burns over most of his upper body, but he's going to be fine, if pretty scarred. A woman named Aida something-or-other was working with him and also got burned up pretty bad.

The weird thing is that his dad says he doesn't remember entering the codes that deactivated the shielding, and neither he nor Aida remembers hearing the alarms until just seconds before the explosion. The doctors say that they may both have some kind of trauma-induced amnesia, but that only explains why they don't remember the alarm, not why they didn't react to it at the time.

Here's another weird thing. It turns out that Aida's daughter, Amneris, is in a band with Olivia. Do you know if maybe Melissa had Olivia steal a hairbrush from Amneris' house? If she did, then all of this might be tied together, even though it's hard for me to see what anyone would have to gain from blowing up an experiment and injuring a bunch of scientists. If you're just going to tell me that everything's going to be okay and I shouldn't worry about it, don't even bother answering that question. I'll save us a bunch of time by assuming stonewalling is your go-to response from here on out.

I think that talking to me was good for Eric. He's really upset, both about his dad getting injured and about not having his phone on when his mom needed him. Maybe my perception is colored a bit because I know that he and I end up falling completely in love, but I think that being able to share his feelings with me really drew us closer, particularly right after he'd been helping me with my depression about my family. Being in public, where we had to worry about what other people think, made holding hands feel intense. In a way, it was more intimate than what we've done when we're alone. In a way.

I'm trying hard to find the bits of hope in everything and trust that it's going to lead to a good place like you say it will. It's not always easy, but this one was pretty good.

BTW, you were right about Olivia and Colin. After school, I saw them walking down the street holding hands. Her eyes looked vacant, like she was a million miles away. More like a PTSD ex-soldier than a love-struck fairytale damsel, though. You know what—I think she made a deal with Melissa. That would explain why I saw her at the shop. I'm thinking that the fire at her house was started because of something Melissa had her do. Melissa hinted she might ask for that kind of thing.

I wonder if Olivia really understood what she was trading for. If that's what actually happened, we're looking at some blackdark Deal with the Devil shit here. I've got some spectacular guilt for the things I've done already, but at least I wasn't directly hurting anyone, and at least I know that it's ultimately supposed to be all for the better. I definitely didn't set out to hurt anyone or do anything with the intent to cause harm. Did she really kill her family to make Colin fall in love with her?

I know; stonewall.

Saturday, May 23

You didn't write back after my last entry but you had told me not to write until Monday, so maybe this is a kind of chastising ignorement because you don't like me using the journal as a diary. I know the pages in this thing are precious and blah, but we still have a bunch left and if I have to keep all of this completely to myself I'm going to explode like a watermelon being pumped full of emotion juice. Writing about it helps.

Mom went in to work today, which is weird for a Saturday. I think it was less about her having a lot to do and more about her wanting to find something to occupy herself beyond brooding around the house.

While Mom was gone, Dad came home and got some things. I was in my room but he didn't come in. It was like we were mutually pretending not to notice the other one was home. As awkward as it was, it was better than having to try and talk to him now that I know where he's been. I really don't want to think about that because skeevie and because it makes me brood about how he could be screwing around when he has to know how much it would hurt me and Mom if we found out.

I do keep thinking that Dad maybe—maybe, maybe, as in the tiniest bit of maybes—might have an inkling of an excuse in his mind for having an affair because

of how screwed and supportless things have been for
him here lately, but the cat lady has no excuse at all.
She's taking advantage of a man who's making a stupid,
hurtful mistake in a time of stress. I wouldn't mind
something appropriately awful happening to her that
makes Dad realize he has to come begging back to Mom.
If you've got a can of cat food I can open somewhere
to make that happen, let me know and I'll be there with
my pull-tab finger primed.

Even though there is so much going on, not being able
to text Eric makes the day seem empty. How weird is
it that I didn't feel this way before we got together?
Losing something is so much worse than never having
had it. I can't wait for the weekend to be over so I
can see him again. I think this is the first time in my
life that I've felt frustrated annoyance about there
being no school on Monday.

Not being able to write doesn't help. I haven't worked
on any of my story or novel ideas since the journal
appeared. My motivation is gone like—like the metaphor
I should have written here. When this is over, I'm going
to really buckle down and get some shit finished and
published. But for now, I haven't got the energy. Writing
fiction seems pathetic with so much actual insanity going
on. "Maybe I'll write a story about a magic puppy that
helps troubled teens find their dreams," I say to myself

while outside some kind of magic portal death magic shit that I helped cause is going on. Yeah, right.

I was Googling around to see if I could find out how Eric's dad is doing. There's an actor named Hector Duran, so that makes it harder to search for him, but if I limit the search to news sites, I get some good hits. The place where he works is called Icon-Higgs, and according to the news the whole facility is on some kind of skeleton-crew lockdown. The official reason is that there's worry about radiation, but some web sites are saying that this makes no sense because the kind of experiments they do involve "neither nuclear materials nor reactions that can be sustained without significant energy input." I think that basically means that if the machine breaks, the experiment will just stop instead of sitting there giving off radiation and creating a race of horrific superpowered mutants.

Hang on—okay, there was just a CNN report saying Eric's family has been moved out of their house and into some kind of quarantine at an "undisclosed location," whatever that means. Some unofficial person is saying that Hector's claim that he didn't intentionally disable the shielding is making "investigators" worry that he may have some kind of mental disease or disorder, or that he might be a "Manchurian candidate of a terrorist organization" (which makes no sense because

Manchurians are Chinese and they aren't terrorists, right?) That same unofficial source says that some smaller explosions have been reported from the lab, but only when people attempt to enter the area where the machine blew up. The news is guessing that if that's true there may have been deaths or injuries that are being covered up, or at least not announced for now. This is really strange. I literally don't understand half of it and don't know what to make of the other half.

I wonder if the quarantine thing means that Eric isn't going to be at school on Tuesday. That has me worried. I wonder if they would let me talk to him if I went to wherever they took his family? I know he's supposed to be grounded, but his parents would have to understand that this is a special situation. I could talk to him through glass or a phone or something, even if he's in quarantine, right? Can you at least tell me where he is?

The lunch you had with Eric, where you sat holding hands and talking, is one of the memories I treasure most. I can still feel the tingle in my fingers sometimes when I go to sleep. Hold on to that memory and treasure it, because it's an anchor you're going to need to tie a serious piece of mental rope to.

Eric is safe. He's in government custody, but it's a decent place, not a prison or anything like that. He and his family can't leave, but they're being taken care of. You aren't going to be able to get anywhere near the facility because it's on a military installation, and I'm not going to tell you where it is because we both know you can't be trusted to stay away. No matter how needy and lonely you feel in the coming days, you can't see Eric until after Melissa has made everything whole again. You know that I'm trapped in the house. If you try to see Eric before you become trapped, either he dies or you are detained and prevented from carrying out our plan, which takes away any possibility of you ever being with him again. I won't let you risk either him or our future together. Don't try to think of some kind of "if you don't let me see Eric I'm going to do [some stupidface thing]" because I'm not moving on this one.

Just so you don't waste time speculating, there have been eighteen additional deaths at Icon-Higgs since the original incident. They aren't due to explosions. The first few were rescue workers killed while searching the site of the disaster for survivors, and the rest were a military team sent in to take down whatever had killed the rescue workers. All of them were killed by the first Patron, which was able to pass into the lab during the disaster. I'm not going to explain what a Patron is before you watch the video tomorrow afternoon.

Write to me after you've seen it and I'll give you more details. We're in the end game here. There should be just a few more days of you having to deal with me. Keep calm, stay detached, obey instructions, and make sure the razor stays on the desk until you need it, and before you know it it will all be over and we'll be free.

Oh, one more thing. The kid who lives next door is going to leave his bicycle on your lawn on Monday morning. We don't want anyone visiting when we're not expecting them, so before you watch the video, put it back in his driveway.

Monday, May 25 (holiday)

You were right about the bike. I moved it. That was random. Moving on...

I don't know what to make of this video. Why do you want me to look at it? It's not my kind of thing and right now I literally can't even imagine what is going on in your head that would make you think I'd want to see this. Are you trying to get me freaked out even more than I already am? Or did someone I know make it?

Whatever. I watched it like you said and I assume you want my reaction. Here's what it looks like to me:

The video is shot like a security video in the showroom of a car dealership. There are a few cars and a desk in the back with a man sitting at it. He's a white guy in a tie.

Another guy comes into the picture from the opposite end of the room from the guy at the desk. This new guy is huge—Dwayne Johnson huge—and covered in a pile of shredded black rags, like he was dressed in a dozen floor-length, oil-soaked hoodies by a clawmangling wolverine. It's impossible to see his head or the shape of his body because of all the rags and because his back is to the camera. I'm going to call this guy Rags and the guy at the desk Tie.

Rags walks up to the desk and puts something on it. I can't really tell what it is because he's far away and the video quality isn't great, but it's some kind of shapeless package, maybe wrapped in newspaper—I'm not sure.

There's no sound, but Tie talks to Rags for a minute, then starts pointing toward the door, like he's telling him to go. Tie seems to be getting frustrated and more and more angry, possibly because Rags isn't responding. Just at the point Tie is starting to get seriously red in the face, another man comes into the room from what looks like the back office. I'm going to call him Boss because that's what he looks like.

Boss goes around the desk to stand next to Rags, grabs his arm, and points emphatically at the door. Rags picks the package up off the desk with the arm that isn't being held and holds it out to Boss. Boss takes it and basically throws it at Rags' chest. It falls to the floor.

Everyone is still for a moment. Rags slowly looks down at the package, then up at Boss and finally over at Tie. That's when things get ridiculous.

I can't really say that Rags exploded then, but that's the closest word I can find. He erupted into a ball of thick, flailing ropes of what looked like solid smoke. The ropes shot out in all directions, and one must have come right at the camera because the screen was filled with black for an instant. Less than a second later, the explosion reversed, sucking back into Rags.

Tie and Boss were gone, but there were massive stains against the back wall that I think we're supposed to think were their smashed bodies, but the stains were dark grey instead of red. I thought it was a problem with the video, because I noticed that an American flag on the wall had grey stripes in the place of the red ones, too. The showroom cars had a similar problem—the ones closest to the desk were a featureless grey, but the ones farther away had both grey and their original color in streaks and spots, as if Rags had detonated a color-sucking paint bomb.

Rags bent down, picked the package up from the floor, and walked slowly out the way he'd come in, his face still hidden by the rags.

Is it a critique of the video you want from me? I'm guessing it's some kind of viral marketing thing for a movie I won't be seeing. The explosion didn't look like anything real, and the color-draining effect makes too little sense to be scary. Am I supposed to do something when this movie comes out? I'm not in the mood.

I watched your video, so it's time for you to pay up. I was thinking about what you said about Melissa contacting patrons (sorry, "Patrons") that were killing people. Are these patrons of her shop? Did these people get something from her that obligated them to be some kind of personal army for her? That makes sense based on what you said about our having to make things go faster to get the world to work together. If she's putting together some kind of slowly growing revolutionary army, I could definitely see world governments arguing about who was responsible for dealing with them until it was too late.

If I'm right about this, I need you to tell me straight up how deep I am into it. Apparently, I got the journal from Melissa's shop; does that make me one of her P/patrons? If they kill people, are you saying that's what I'm going to turn into? Is that what happened to Olivia? Have you trapped yourself inside the house because if you leave you'll become homicidal? I admit I've been in a near-constant state of panic and depression lately, but the last thing I want to do is kill anyone. Is that going to change?

Answering your last question first, yes, you are going to start feeling like killing someone, and you need to rein in any feelings like that as soon as you notice even a hint of them. Your temper and impulsiveness got us where I am, and the only way out of it is for you to be as detached and clinical about all of this as possible, no matter how bad it gets. Your springtrigger violence has nothing to do with Melissa and everything to do with your inability to control yourself.

Aside from that, every speculation and conclusion in your last entry is wrong. I told you not to waste your time with that.

The Patrons aren't people; they're things from another dimension/world/place—I'm not sure what the right thing to call it is. The video is completely real, and "Rags" is the first Patron to have made it into our world. The explosion at Icon-Higgs opened the door, and that's what walked through.

Patrons aren't people. They aren't even thinking creatures in the normal sense. This one and the ones that come after it are mindlessly following threads of outsider energy and attempting to gather it. I can't give you a lot of details because I barely understand them myself, but the Patrons follow the energy until they find a person, then they offer the person something. If the person gives the Patron something with the energy in it, the trade is complete and the Patron goes away. If the trade is refused or not completed to the Patron's satisfaction—you saw the kind of thing that happens. To make it even more complicated, the Patrons don't speak or write, so there's no way to know what it is they want to trade for. These things are so far outside our experience that it's pointless to even try and find the reason in them.

What the Patrons offer to trade also seems nonsensical. I think it's something they happen to see that they think is valuable or beautiful, based on whatever sense of wealth or aesthetics they have. I've seen a few things they've offered and they range from the baffilyingly common—an egg, a beer mug—to the horrifying—a dog's snout and worse.

I don't know what it was at the car dealership that would have satisfied the Patron. It could have been anything or anyone that was near the explosion at Icon-Higgs, an object that Melissa or someone like her interacted with, something that was bathed in the light from Mom's ceremony, or I could be guessing completely wrong and it's something else entirely. I don't know what "outsider energy" really is, what it looks like, or how someone would go about finding or even detecting it. That means that every trade with a Patron is effectively a game of Russian roulette with a death penalty for non-participation.

They can sense people and have no concern for barriers or sight lines. If they sense someone they want to make a trade with, they relentlessly, sleeplessly keep after that person until an offer can be made. Resistance is pointless. Patrons don't seem to notice if they're shot or gassed. They interpret attacks with any kind of weapon to be an attempted trade. They seem puzzled by anyone kicking them but relentlessly hunt down and crush anyone who attacks them with fists. If one is trapped, it explodes with increasing frequency and force until it is free.

The Patrons are so strange and awful that it's easier for governments to speculate and point fingers than do anything about one or ten or a dozen of them walking around. But if

Melissa can release a flood of them, the world will fight back soon enough to thwart genocide.

There are only a few things left for you to do to complete our work, but they are some of the most difficult. After Mom goes to bed, get her safety deposit key out of her purse. Tomorrow, school is going to be cancelled around 9 o'clock, so don't bother going. Instead, go to the bank at 10:30, get in Mom's safety deposit box, and bring everything in it home. Let me know when you have it.

That's insane. Literally, LITERALLY insane. You keep pushing and pushing me, asking me to believe yet another impossible thing and think that somehow I'm going to just accept it and meet your constant demands with blind trust. I only accepted that you were me because I can't think of any other explanation for what you know, but if you were me then you'd know that I should have been way past my limit a long time ago.

I don't know how this journal works, but it does. I can't deny that, no matter how bad I want to. It's the same with the shitfucked things you ask me to do—I doubt and I push back, but you keep being right about things you have no right to be right about. Now you want me to believe that there are rag monsters from another dimension that explode into murder if you don't trade trinkets with them? That's orders of magnitude more unbelievable than anything you've fed me so far. That's "an imaginary tree is dating a hat that was once your grandfather" territory. We've finally gotten to the point that it's more likely you're making shit up than what you say is true, no matter how much evidence you bring to the table.

I think Mom would die a little inside if she heard me say it, but I don't believe in magic. When I was small, she would tell me stories before I went to sleep, sitting in the nightlight glow beside my bed. On a few occasions, after telling some tale of fairies, she would remind me that magic was real, then reach up into the darkness and pull a red, glowing spot of light out of it, holding it delicately between finger and thumb. It would be there for just a moment, then she would blow on it and open her fingers and it would be gone. When I asked her how it worked, she said it was magic, "just like the coven and I chase every week."

Years later, I was putting laundry away and found a little device buried under her socks. It was a thing you could hide in your hand to make a pinpoint of light. They even sell them on Amazon. I confronted her with the proof that her magic light was just a deception and she said, "But the magic WAS real—it was in your heart and mind all along." This was our family's version of learning that there is no Santa Claus.

If you really are me, then you remember it too. I learned all at once that magic wasn't real and that Mom had deeply devoted her life to something she had to know in her heart was a lie. You had me for a while with the thing at Mom's coven, but I'm convinced now that there's some normal explanation that I'm just too ignorant to figure out. There is no magic. No matter how long I live, I'm not going to forget that again.

I've been playing your game because I really don't have a choice. There's definitely something going on that I can't explain, and whenever I don't play by its rules, horrible things happen. I don't believe you're me anymore because I'd know you were asking too much of me. I don't believe these "Patrons" are magic, but I found articles online about the car dealership and a later thing at a grocery store where 15 people died, so I know that they're something horrible, no matter what they are.

I don't know how Melissa does it, but she's a master manipulator of some kind. You might be her, you might be someone under her control, I don't know. The one thing I do know is that the risk of things getting worse if I don't play along seems to be very real. I'm like a Bible character doing something I've been commanded to do not because I think it's right but because if I don't a vengeful God will rain fire on my people.

You better hope I don't figure a way out of this game, because when I do I'm going, and I'm going in a way that will do you as much harm as possible.

By the way, here's another piece of evidence: if you were really me you'd know that the bank thing isn't going to work. You have to sign or have a code or something to get into the box at the bank. They aren't going to let me in. You've written yourself into a corner.

Soon, very soon, you will change your mind about magic. You—and I really am you—will get to the point that only your faith in magic keeps you moving through the day because only magic can give you back what has been taken from you. Eric is out there waiting for me, and only Melissa's magic can free me to go to him.

I remember Mom's trick with the light, and I remember how devastated I felt when I found it in the back of the drawer, under her zebra socks, hidden away like a shameful secret she couldn't bear to rid herself of. This isn't the same. I've seen the world crawling with Patrons. I've seen the power in Melissa's magic. I've even seen what happens when Mom finally releases the true magic that has eluded her all these years. When you're on my end, writing the replies in this journal, you will be deep in acceptance. You will have no choice.

Here's another bit of proof for you: you're wrong about the bank. By tomorrow morning, the Patron will have killed seven more on a public bus and baseless rumors about terrorist attacks, mass hysteria, and radiation from Icon-Higgs will have people in a panic. The bank is going to be a madhouse of people scrambling to bag their cash and valuables so they can get out of town as quickly as possible. Between the chaos and certain other things that have been put in motion, you'll get into the box with no problem.

If anyone asks, say that Mom sent you to get your things because she's too busy packing. Given the situation, it'll be believable.

Keep your head. Don't look nervous or do anything suspicious and you'll be fine. Trust me. Trust *you*.

Tuesday, May 26

Seven died on a bus overnight. I am fighting so hard against believing that you're telling the truth but you keep predicting shit like that. I want so bad for you to be a liar because if you're telling the truth it's the most horrible thing imaginable.

I'll do your damned errand.

I got the key from Mom's purse, no problem. There was a bottle of pills in there that I didn't recognize. I looked them up online, and they're for depression. I wish I knew how long she'd been taking them; I was clueless that things were that bad. I'm glad I didn't tell her about where Dad is. I hope she doesn't know. I wish I could stop thinking about the pills.

I didn't want to raise any suspicions this morning so I went to school anyway, even though you said it would be let out early. Surprise—you were right about that. Instead of just letting us go they wanted any students who didn't have cars to wait for a parent to come pick them up because they didn't want to let us walk home. I couldn't call Mom because I didn't want her knowing what I was doing and I really can't face Dad right now. I don't know if I'll ever be able to look him in the eye again without seeing a stranger. I wish the fucking cat lady had been hit by a fucking truck.

There's some of that anger you keep telling me to keep in check. Maybe you just need to learn to deal with it and let me be myself.

I found a guy who had a car and agreed to give me a ride for $20. He wanted another $20 when I said I wanted to be dropped off at the bank. Does panic turn everyone into an Uber driver or something? That's your spirit of selfless cooperation right there.

Here's where you can insert the "I told you so" about how I would have saved $40 if I'd stayed home. Here, I'll even leave space for you to write it:

If you're really from the future, I should be able to turn the page after I write this entry and then turn back to see what you've written in that space. Good luck getting out of that one.

What are you doing? This is where everything comes together. Don't play with it; don't do anything that can risk messing it up.

I don't know what would happen if I inserted something on a page you already wrote. I can't think of any time path where that would make sense, so my trying a stunt like that would either break the system or throw us into a loop until I didn't do it. I'm not going to even try and at this point you should be smart enough not to even ask.

Quit being a shitbrain. Tell me what happened at the bank.

Why should I? You're me, right? You were there. Tell
yourself.

You don't want to play my games? Well, I don't want
to play yours, either. You insist that you're me from
the future, but—impossible knowledge aside—you act
like a stranger. I would never make myself go through
what I'm going through if I had a choice. You want me
to play your games, you have to come clean. No more
bullshit. Sorry—am I repeating myself?

It's never been about bullshit. There are things I haven't told you, but I've never lied to you without a completely justifiable reason.

The details—even the smallest ones—of what we are doing are so important that I can't rely on my memory. I know I've forgotten things and I know that my pain interferes with my thinking sometimes. I also have some blurs in my past because of those pills you found in Mom's purse. I took them, too many at a time, for a while to try and chemical myself out of what the world was doing to me, and overdosing followed by sudden cold turkey when they ran out screwed me up. Do us a both a favor and get rid of them while you still can.

There are things I'm holding back because I think that telling you them might cause you to make a mistake or not follow my directions. I might be wrong about that. It's hard for me to be objective because my old attitude—your attitude—did so much damage.

Things feel impossible from where I am. I remember your tonight very well. It's one of the most important nights in this whole business and it changed my perspective on everything forever. I remember being mad at my future self, I remember demanding answers, I remember thinking that if I wasn't satisfied I was going to trash the whole business and fuckall the consequences. I remember my future self breaking down and telling me something that she was keeping hidden, then wishing I hadn't heard it and spending hours in a sweat-drenched near-panic waiting to experience what I was told was coming.

Most importantly, I remember making a small mistake that scarred my memory, but blessedly not screwing up the part that meant the most.

I'm running from my memories here. I don't want you to make that small mistake, but maybe I have to just give up and let my old self make it. If I try to keep things hidden to avoid the small one, perhaps a larger one will take its place.

Here's what we'll do. Go over what happened at the bank so I know for certain where we stand. After you do that, I'll tell you some of what you want to know. Later, Mom is going to go out for the evening and I'll tell you more—a lot more.

You can't let go of being controlling, can you? Not even when you say you're going to stop hiding things from me. If you can't trust me, how am I supposed to trust you?

Fine. You'll tell me your little secret, I'll show you I'm not so stupid that I'll screw things up even when you tell me I'm going to and we can stop playing this game. I bet I can even avoid turning into a drug addict without throwing away the medication my mother needs to deal with the crap in her life. Maybe you don't remember this, but I've been wearing grown-up pants for a while now.

So, the bank.

The bank was full-on "free rage-inducing drugs day at the asylum," crammed with people trying to get more cash than they could from the ATM or do other panic banking.

It took me more than an hour to get through the line to a teller to ask about getting into the safety deposit box, and when I did they just sent me to another line over around the side near the vault. That one was shorter, at least.

While I waited, I tried to shut out the noise of people yelling at tellers so I could mentally rehearse my story for why I wanted to get into the box without Mom. So many people were talking about grabbing valuables and getting out of town that I didn't think I'd have any trouble making a case that we were doing the same. Lots of people weren't even going into the little room with their box, but just dumping its contents into a bag or purse and getting out of there as quickly as possible.

I thought that maybe they'd stop checking ID or something because of the situation and that's why you were so certain I'd be able to get in, but they didn't. I even saw one person who had to be taken out of the building by security because she was trying to get into a box that wasn't hers. Then, after I'd been in the second line for a bit, I noticed that Patrick was one of the people processing the safety-deposit line.

It was surreal. What was a high-school student doing working in a bank and on a weekday? It made no sense. When I got to the front of the line, he recognized me right off.

I handed him the box key and he asked for my ID. I gave it to him.

"You work here?" I asked.

"I have a free period so I normally leave school early and work for a few hours in the afternoon, as a work-experience thing. They called me when they heard school was canceled because they needed all hands to deal with the rush." He checked something on the computer, double-checked my ID, and gave me a tight-lipped look like he was trying to decide what to do. "Your parents send you here to clear out their box?"

I nodded. "We're going out of town."

He pushed the key and my ID back to me. "Type in the access code," he said, nodding toward a keypad on the counter near me.

"I don't—" He cut me off, apparently guessing what I was going to say.

"There's a long line," he said. "Just type the code." He looked at me intensely, making his words insistent.

I typed garbage into the keypad.

He thanked me and buzzed me through the half-height door into the vault area. Another teller was finishing up with a customer and went to take the next person in line.

Patrick led me into the vault, took my key again, and opened a safety deposit box using my key and one of his own. "They usually don't let me work in the vault unaccompanied," he said as he pulled the drawer out of its slot. "You lucked out. Another teller wouldn't have let you in, even if your parents had remembered to give you the code. I owe you one for the other day, though. I don't know why you did that, but it helped. You didn't just defuse the situation with the bullies, you showed me that

not everyone is as uncaring as those assholes. It really
made a difference."

That made me smile. For a minute, I actually thought
good thoughts about you because you had shown me how
to help this guy. Then I realized that this moment was
the only reason you'd done it. You weren't helping a guy
being bullied; you were helping me rob a bank.

Patrick held the box while I put everything in a Ziploc
and stashed it in my backpack. He warned me not to
try getting in a bank that way again, we said a round of
mutual thanks, and I left.

When I got home, there were wards scried on all the
windows and doors. Mom's home, but she's at her altar
and I know better than to interrupt her so I can't
ask what exactly they are, but I can guess. She obviously
thinks something supernatural is going on and has a
plan to protect us from it. Believe me, I'll be asking
her about it when she's done. The time for my passively
sitting in the dark, letting other people run the world all
around me, is over.

Until then: I've got the Ziploc here. There's a bunch of
envelopes, some passports, a jewelry box, and a big old
strike-anywhere matchbox that's heavy and taped shut.
I didn't open anything so I wouldn't risk pissing you off.

Now what.

The papers are the usual licenses and insurance documents. There is some private stuff in there of Mom and Dad's that you'll feel better not going into, but I'm not going to even try recommending that you leave them alone, what with your adult pants and all. Put the papers somewhere safe and out of sight because you won't be able to put them back in the bank even if you want to. In a week, the bank's not even going to be there.

The matchbox is filled with old silver coins. I still have those and am going to make good use of them when I'm able to get out of the house. Precious metals are really handy right now.

You're going to think about opening the matchbox and dumping the lot through the heater grate in the hall to "teach me a lesson" for bossing you around so much. Don't. You'll only end up going after them later and it's gross in there. Just put the whole box in a drawer or something.

The most important thing right now is the jewelry box. There's a locket and chain inside. The locket is completely unique. Push on the top to open the locket's lid, which opens down from the top, then push on the bottom to open the inner lid, which opens up from the bottom. Inside is a tiny piece of rough cloth embroidered with a pentangle. The cloth is actually woven from human hair, and each strand is from a different person. I don't know whose, and I don't know where the red thread of the embroidery came from.

Once you've satisfied your curiosity, close the pendant, wrap the chain a few times around your left wrist, and wear it like an awkward bracelet until Mom notices it and asks you for it. Give it to her. She won't ask how you got it.

After Mom has the locket, she's going to leave the house. Tell me when she does and how it went and I'll give you some of the answers you want.

"Completely unique"? Really? Have I forgotten in my old age that that's redundant? You'd think I'd have learned the lesson by then. You know, your writing style is very close to mine. That's more something I'd expect from someone copying my writing than I'd expect from myself in the future. Curious I don't develop in writing the way I apparently do in attitude. When we get to our Q+A, I'll be interested to see how you explain that one.

By the way, if you're going to tell me not to do something, don't have a paragraph break between my inspiration and your warning. When I read that you needed the coins, I went and dumped them in the heater grate. I didn't see your next paragraph until I got back. There now, I've taught you something. I'm sure I'll be remembering that lesson when "I" go and dig through the dust in the wall for those coins later.

Mom still hasn't come in. I feel like an idiot sitting in my room with a locket around my wrist. There's an *explodetraders tag trending on Twitter with news about your "Patrons." I can't tell if it's still the one or if there is more than one at this point, but there have been two more attacks this evening. I really need a crapless explanation of what these things are and I'm pretty certain I haven't gotten one yet. That's going to be Q+A item *2.

While we're enjoying our new honesty, I'm going drop the pretense and start calling you Melissa. You gave it a good shot, but your aim just isn't that good. I'm giving you until the morning, and if you haven't given me a good reason by then, I'm dropping this whole "magic journal" thing and finding a way to get to Eric. You keep using him as a carrot to get me to do what you want, but I bet he isn't as hard to get to as you want me to believe.

I wonder how well you'd do if I went online and told literally everyone about you? I bet you and your magic terrorist friends would rather avoid that kind of scrutiny, wouldn't you?

Just thinking out loud while I wait for Mom. Don't pay any attention to little old me.

What the fuck is this? I'm going through the papers from the safety box and there are birth and death certificates for a baby named Perdita, born three months after my parents were married and died three days later. What are you trying to convince me of with that? If it were real, my parents would have told me, and if you didn't want me to find it, you wouldn't have made such a big point of pointing out that there were "secrets" in the papers.

Do you expect me to go on about "how could you possibly have planted something in my parents' safety deposit box?" I know all too well that you have ways to get things done that are too clever for me to figure out. At some point, you stop trying to explain magic tricks and just accept that no matter how hard you try you can be fooled by a professional.

You are so God-damned manipulative, but I'm on guard now. I'm not

Diana (Petulia):

The amulet is the key. It can multiply a hundredfold any Earth energies its holder encounters. Take it where you sent the light and cast a Welcoming.

Mom's gone with the locket and you have more explaining to do than you have ever had in your life.

She walked in while I was writing. I was so engrossed in it that I didn't even hear her coming. There was no way I could hide the journal.

When I looked up, she was standing in my doorway, staring right at the damned thing sitting on my desk with my pen poised over a paragraph claiming she had a dead baby. I didn't know what to do. The look in her eyes—like she had been surprised by a long-lost childhood friend who was somehow still a child—was a Medusa stare that made a statue out of me.

"Is that—" she asked, letting her own question trail off. She stepped into the room and reached for the journal. I just dropped the pen to the side and rolled the chair back from the desk.

Mom half-closed the book so she could see the cover without lifting the journal from the desk, then lay it open again and turned the page. I thought that was the end of everything, that turning the page would count as looking ahead and break the journal completely. I surprised myself by having a moment of panic at the thought of losing this thing instead of a blast of relief of being freed from my burden. I was falling into the water, worrying that the rope holding the millstone around my neck might come loose.

Mom saw the message on the next page, addressed to her and using the nickname Grandma had for her. I didn't know what it meant, but Mom obviously did. She looked from it to me, wide-eyed, then said, "We should talk," and walked out of the room. I followed.

She went to the living room and sat on the couch, patting the cushion for me to sit beside her. Then she just started talking.

"When I was little," she said, "Mom—Grandma Kay— kept that book in her altar. She called it 'Tomorrow's Journal,' and said that any time she needed help, she'd write her problems in there and it would guide her with the turn of a page. That book was the greatest taboo in the house. She kept it wrapped in a dozen thick rubber bands and forbade us to so much as touch it. I didn't see the bands on your desk."

"I use binder clips," I said, half surprising myself that I'd said anything. The conversation was ten steps past surreal.

Mom nodded. "That's sensible. More modern."

She sat quietly for a moment, looking at her hands, then started talking without looking up. "When I was ten I wanted to go to summer camp on Catalina. Mom said I couldn't because Tomorrow's Journal said so, and I was so mad I didn't speak a word for three days. I was convinced she was using the book as an excuse for not wanting to shell out the money, and I began forming secret plans to make her life a living hell for the two summer weeks my friends were off enjoying the island and I was stuck at home.

"A month later, my friends were all away and I was three days into my passive-aggressive parent-annoying shit fest when we got the news that two of my best friends had been flown back from Catalina and were in the hospital. They'd snuck out at night to visit a place where wild boars nested and tried to pick up some piglets that they thought were alone. They were attacked by adults that heard the babies squeal and were both seriously injured. They lived, but with scars and, for one of them, a permanent limp. If I'd been at camp, I'd have gone with them. No question about it."

Mom looked up from her hands. "When I was nearing graduation from high school, I asked Mom to ask the journal where I should go to college. She said the journal said UCLA, which sounded boring to me because it was so close to home. I applied everywhere I could think of that I might want to go, but only UCLA accepted me.

"Right around the time you were born, Mom stopped getting answers from the journal. I was well into the magic by then and had accepted the journal for what Mom said it was, but when I asked her to see your future in it, she said she couldn't. She still wrote in it now and then, but said that the time had come for it to stop writing to her, so she had to write for it. I didn't know what that meant and I still don't. You were only a toddler when she passed across, and I thought that when I inherited her altar I'd finally get to open the journal and release its secrets. But when I went to look for it, it was gone. I assumed Mom had hidden it when she knew her end was coming and that it would turn up when I most needed it, but it never did. At least, not for me.

"I'm not going to ask how you got the journal or Grandma Kay's locket. She could do things alone with her altar that I can't do with my whole coven at my side. I'm a girl with a squirt gun whose mother was a firefighter. If those things have found their way to you, then Grandma Kay wants you to have them and I'm not going to second-guess. If you've kept them secret, it's because they are secrets by nature and I've no right to ask you to give up their power. If you've read the journal, you already know everything Grandma learned from it—Catalina, my college, how she met Grandpa, how he had to die, a near-drowning, a dead pet, a new job, and probably dozens of things that were never shared with me because they weren't meant to be.

"Here's a funny thing. About a month ago I went into this new occult-supply shop—the place where I found that bowl I told you about—and got to talking with the owner about the Coven, about Grandma Kay, about you. It was so nice to talk so freely about what I loved with someone I'd never met before, and she had such a genuine interest it warmed my heart. Just being in that shop brought me a peace and calm I haven't felt in a long time. I wanted you to experience it for yourself, but without my influence, so I took one of their business cards and dropped it into your backpack so that you'd come across it some time when the stars were smiling. A little bit of serendipity. I was hoping that seeing all the wonderful things and talking with someone closer to your age might spark your interest in the craft, not knowing that you were already so far beyond me. I can't tell you how proud I am."

She took a deep breath and let it out slowly. "I suppose I should have asked before turning the page, but when I saw the book, I felt like it was calling to me. I am so lost in the currents right now that I don't know what to do. Your dad's turned into a man I don't even know, a thing that must be from across the plane of separation is loose in this world, and there's an ache in my heart that I'm at fault but don't know how or what I can do about it. The journal was a flash of hope, and when I reached for it, there it was—the answer with a turn of a page, just like Mom said. I could feel her speaking to me, just as she must be speaking to you."

We sat in silence for a second, then Mom asked if she could see the locket. I unwound the chain from my wrist and poured it into her hand. She opened it with practiced fingers.

"Grandma Kay had this locket made," she said, "but the work inside is centuries old. She wore it always. You can see the chain in almost every picture of her we have, but she usually had the locket itself against her chest, hidden from view. After she died, I wore it for a while, thinking that it would help me with my magics the way it helped her, but it didn't. It eventually became a reminder of something I could never be, so I put it away. It was in our safety deposit box, in fact. I don't know how it found its way to you, but little mysteries remind me that there is a greater purpose working in the world so I have no interest in trying to work them out."

She closed the locket. "The journal says I need this. May I borrow it?" I nodded, even though it felt weird that I was giving Mom permission to take something that was by all rights hers in the first place.

There was another minute of silence with Mom just staring at the locket and turning it over and over in her hand. It was weird that she was making so little eye contact when she usually makes so much that it's almost exhausting. Finally, she said, "I always knew that you had the talent in you and that it would come forward someday. That's why I never pushed you to start learning the craft. Besides, I'm not sure there's much I could really teach you.

"My coven's a farce. I think you've probably guessed that by now. The ceremonies really are based on ancient magic, but in our unspoken hearts we all know it's an excuse and the feelings of oneness have more to do with making ourselves feel the way any religion makes its true believers feel than with drawing in energy from the universe. The sex rituals weren't about intimacy or love but about trying to explore the magic energies in the world around us. It wasn't even real sex, just simulated— no, not even that. It was just symbolic, so there's no reason for your dad to feel threatened by it. I thought he understood that, but recently—I don't even know.

"You probably don't want to hear about that," she said, giving me a weak smile before going back to looking at the amulet. "I kept telling myself we were making the world a better place. You can understand that, right?"

I said yes because there was nothing else I could say, but am not sure it would have made a difference if I hadn't said a word.

"I think where I went wrong," she continued, "was forgetting so much of what Grandma had raised me to believe in and letting myself get wrapped up in worrying about material wealth and personal success. I think that's what has led me to ruin everything so completely. If I had stayed pure, maybe I could have been like Grandma in the craft and really had a connection to the substance of the Earth.

"The other night, when the coven created that beam of light, was the only time we've accomplished something substantial, but at the moment it occurred I wasn't thinking about empowering the earth. I was thinking about punishing someone or, more specifically, about using magic to gather great wealth as an 'I told you so' to anyone who had doubted me. I only had that negative thought for a moment, but it was at that moment that the wonder occurred. I know now that it wasn't a coincidence. In a moment of weakness, I let something horrible through.

"You've probably seen the video of the thing at the Ford dealership. I think the coven is responsible for that. We created it, or attracted it, or made an opening for it to come through—I honestly don't know which. Now it's killing people because a group of middle-aged fools were getting off on playing Wicca and not paying proper respect to the forces we were toying with."

This time when Mom looked up, she held my gaze and there was a little bit of the old steel in her eyes. She gestured with the amulet. "This is what I needed to make it right again. The journal has pointed me in the right direction. With Grandma Kay's strength behind me, I can send that thing back where it came from. I know it. I can feel it in my spirit all the way to the soles of my feet.

"I'm going to go out for a little while. I've put wards on the house so that if that thing comes near it will pass by as if the house didn't exist, and even if it is able to see through them it won't be able to do so much as knock on the door. You will be entirely safe until I get back, and when I do get back it will be with our troubles wrapped up and composted. You and I are going to do great things. I can feel it. Are you ready for that?"

I nodded like I was supposed to. Through the whole conversation, the more details Mom gave me the more I became convinced that she didn't know what she was talking about. She was blaming herself for things Melissa had done, or maybe I had done, but there was no way I could stop and correct her without having to explain so many things that either I didn't understand or that would make me sound insane.

Literally lost in the weird moment, unsure what to do, I heard myself saying something I'd been reminding myself not to say: "Mom, who was Perdita?"

Mom's face fell, like she just realized she'd been poisoned. "Is she talking to you?" she asked. "Do you hear spirits like Grandma used to?"

That caught me by surprise to the point that my tongue remained knotted into immobility. Mom apparently took this as confirmation.

"Tell her I'm sorry," she said. "I didn't want to bring her into the world, and I think that's why the world didn't let me keep her. I never would have hurt her. We did everything we could to do right by her. But in my heart, I wasn't ready, so she came too soon and then couldn't stay. Your baby sister—your big sister, really— never made it home from the hospital."

She stood up. "I have to go. Grandma has reached back through her journal and shown me how to redeem myself." She hugged me, kissed me on the cheek. "I love you and I always will. We're going to get through this, and when we do, I'm going to start giving you the attention you deserve."

Mom hugged me again, maybe a little too tight, then grabbed her traveling kit, jacket, and car keys and disappeared into the garage. I didn't move from the couch until after I heard her drive away.

So now what? That's got to be enough detail, even for you. Is this where we have the big reveal? You're not me from the future but really my dead magic grandma come back to guide me from the spirit world, or writing to me from the past, or some bullshit like that? I tell you right now I won't believe it. Mom does; not me. It's too movie-poetic-perfect.

By the time I realized it might have been better to stop Mom than to let her do whatever it was that the message you wrote her made her think to do, it was too late. Given everything that happened, I can only assume that it's going to make things worse, not better. I'll tell you this right now: if Mom doesn't come back, if something happens to her, if you sent her into a trap, I will kill you. If you made me part of something horrible that is going to happen to her, then I don't care how much magic you have, I will find a way. I will cut out your fucking heart.

I'm not Grandma Kay, I'm you. Just like I've been telling you. If Mom's right that this journal is the same one Grandma used, then she must have written to herself the same way you are writing to yourself. That's how she knew the future. Her writing isn't there anymore because anything written in the book eventually disappears. That's why when it was time for me to write the responses to you, only your writing remained. My writing—the words you are reading right now—has been in the book the longest so it's the first to disappear. After I've written it, your writing will disappear so the book can be sent back for you to fill in.

I didn't want you to find out about Perdita because I'd be happier never knowing about her. I had to tell you not to look in the papers in a vague way that might stop you, but that didn't reveal what was in them so that if you were dissuaded from looking I would never form the memory I don't want to have. If you'd trusted me, you wouldn't have looked. Because you didn't trust me, you did look, and that gave Mom the opportunity to prove to you that I wasn't lying. When you're really ready to wallow in it, there's a shoebox in the back of Mom and Dad's closet shelf tied with a ribbon so brittle it's broken under its own weight. There are things in there, most of them never used, that will rip at the seams of your soul, including a map with an X marking a graveyard plot that you will never have a chance to visit if you insist on getting in our way.

Now, please, say that you have enough evidence that I am who I say I am that you can trust me. Soon, very soon, things will be dire. I need your trust.

Wait, there's more? I thought the whole conversation with Mom was the thing you were warning me I had to be careful not to screw up. Isn't this enough? Do you see me as some kind of bottomless resource motivated by heart tugs? How can you keep asking me to do these things?

First, though, and most importantly, you're avoiding the question about Mom. What happens to her tonight? Does she destroy the Patron or the gate it came in through or whatever? Is she okay?

I'm going to be completely straightforward because that's all that seems to come even close to working.

Mom fails. She finds her way into Icon-Higgs, goes into the room where the Patron came through, and uses the amulet to cast a spell. Or, rather, she tries to cast one. Mom expects the amulet to increase the power of her Welcome, which should draw natural Earth energy to her and repair the damage that's been done. Instead, the amulet augments the strongest force in the area, which is the portal spell Melissa arranged.

There's something coming soon I need you to do. Write when it's full dark.

Why are you burying the most important part of this?
Mom's in trouble and we're sitting here journaling about
it? Fuck this. I'm going to stop her.

Damn you to hell. The tires on my car are all slashed. I
can't get an Uber, the taxi places aren't even answering
their phone, and it would be impossible for me to walk
to the Higgs place in time to save Mom. I don't know
how you did it, but you stopped me. You literally made
it impossible for me to save my own mother. I would
never do that. I would never, never, never do that. Fuck
you for saying you're me.

I am you. I would never have let Mom put herself in danger if there was a way around it, but there is no way.

I still can't remember the name of that kid next door, but he was watching from his bedroom window when you moved his bicycle, and a little later his dad backed over it in their car. The tire slashing was his misplaced revenge.

I'm sorry I stopped you from going after Mom but I had to. If you reached her at Icon-Higgs what would you do? Tell her that you want to stop her from trying to save the world by undoing what she thinks she's done to harm it? How could you convince her that she's wrong? You couldn't. All you could do is get yourself in the way, probably ruin the spell, and maybe get yourself killed by a Patron.

I don't know what happens to Mom after the spell fails. All Melissa would tell me is that she's alive, but from what I have learned from Mom's books, I think that because she was holding the amulet her spell would have worked just enough to hold her safe. I think she's probably trapped at Icon-Higgs in the contaminated room. If she is, I think I know how to save her, but I can't do that until I can get out of the house. You're the only one who can help me with that. You're the only one who can save her now.

Well, if Melissa says Mom is fine then I guess it's all hunky peachpie dory, isn't it? We all trust Melissa so much around here she's practically our patron saint. You'd know that better than me, of course.

If you aren't letting me do anything for Mom—and I want to make it perfectly clear that I'm fully aware you aren't—you have to tell me everything you know about what happened. Is what Mom did the thing that makes the situation worse so that the world can "pull together" and solve the problem? Is everything back to normal by your time? And when are you going to tell me why you are trapped in the house and how I'm supposed to save you?

You promised answers. Give.

Fine. It's dark here, pretty much all the time. The Patrons are everywhere, but people have learned how not to set them off. I don't know the details because the Patrons leave me alone. For everyone else it's a weird, delicate existence, like living in a global prison camp where you have to time all your moves to avoid the guards and searchlights.

The rent in space at Icon-Higgs was the first and Mom bringing the amulet there both made it the biggest and helped it open others all around the world. That's the burst that gets people to pull together. In a real way, Mom's the hero here.

In my time, Patrons still come through, but not nearly as often as they used to. People in every country are working together toward a solution, and there are high hopes that within five years they will have one that can completely eliminate the rents and the Patrons.

Melissa—I can't even describe what she has become. I haven't seen her since the last time you saw her, but she communicates with me when necessary. She's everything she wanted to become, I guess, and aside from me and a few others she leaves everyone alone now. When you and I are done, she's promised to make me like we used to be again.

That's all I need to leave the house. I need to be like you are. Healthy. Full of life. I'm horribly crippled because of a mistake you make. I can't tell you what it was because I have a strong feeling that if I do, you'll just make a worse mistake—one that can't be repaired, or that leaves me so weak that I can't use the journal.

We can save Mom. We can find Eric.

The time is coming very soon. You'll need the razor. Keep it close. Tell me when dark falls.

If you really are me, how far in the future are you?
If you can't tell me exactly, can you tell me in years or
decades?

My sense of time is screwed up because I'm never sure how long I sleep and nothing that can tell me the date works. I don't see people, and if I did I can't talk to them. I don't think the seasons are acting the way they should, but even if they were, California weather is a crap calendar.

The best I can estimate, I'm five or six months from you.

That's five or six months of nearly constant pain, of not knowing what happened to Eric or Mom, of being trapped in a prison of my own stupidity. Without you, I'm facing an eternity of the same.

You're my only hope and my only hope hates me, doesn't trust me, and won't listen to me even when I'm trying to save her life. Think about that. Think about the hell I'm in.

No more until full dark. When the sun's gone from your window, let me know. Before then, please just let me be.

The sun's down. Just a second after it disappeared behind the hills there was a loud noise and a blue flash, like a power transformer exploded. I can't see anything and the power's still on. Is that what you were waiting for?

That was Mom. The little tear is now a huge rent, and in about six hours Patrons are going to be pouring through.

Don't even think about asking questions for a few minutes. There is about to be a knock on the door, and when you hear it it is extremely important that you do everything EXACTLY, precisely as I'm about to describe it. Read these instructions over and keep reading them over until you hear the knock. This is CRITICAL.

- When you hear the knock, pick up the box of aluminum foil and go immediately to the front door without hesitation.

- There will be five slow knocks on the door, then about ten seconds of silence before the knocks start again. Open the door during the silence, before the knocks restart. If you are too late, wait for another five knocks and open the door during the silence.

- Keep your eyes down and don't look at the person at the door.

- You will be handed a small package wrapped in newspaper. Trade it for the box of foil.

- Don't say anything.

- Close the door.

- DO NOT open the package. Immediately go out back and throw it as hard as you can over the back fence so you can't easily get to it even if you got curious. You DO NOT want to know what is in the package and I'm not going to tell you so don't ask. This is worse than finding Dad. This is worse than anything you might guess. This is not a reverse-psychology trick to get you to open the thing. DO NOT open the package.

- Tell me, in detail, what happened. My memories stop for about two days from about this point so I need to know.

You sick bitch! What is wrong with you? What is wrong with everything?

You knew there were a baby's hands in that package. Curled into little fists. One stump cut clean, one ragged like it was torn off. So small, damp in bloody newspaper. I fell to the tile after fumbling it open and just clutched the poor things to my chest, screaming myself raw and choking on tears and snot.

It was Emilia. I recognize the burn on the finger. That thing murdered the Atkinsons' baby and you wanted me to throw the evidence away. What the fuck kind of monster are you? I tried to call the police but the phone and my cell phone are out and the internet is down with them.

It was one of your Patrons at the door. I looked it right in the face and there was no face there, just flaps of black flesh that moved in a breeze that I couldn't feel. It took the foil and walked off down the street, but I'm afraid to go to a neighbor or even to yell for help because I don't know if it will come back. It killed a baby, a little baby.

How can you be so calm about that? Why didn't you try to stop it???

~~I tried to stop it. I told you not to babysit that day, but you did anyway. At that point, you weren't any more trusting than you are now and you're so paranoid and headstrong that if I'd said, "If you babysit at the Atkinsons' tonight their baby is going to be murdered" you would have assumed I'm insane and never listened to another thing I said.~~

~~The Patron is following an energy trail you've left because of your involvement with magic. The trail led to the Atkinsons' because you wouldn't listen to me. You could have spared me months of nightmares about unwrapping the package to find those little fists if you'd listened. Why can't you follow a single shitsimple instruction? Your temper and bullheadedness are completely fucking everything up. What do I have to say to convince you that all of this mindless ranting and paranoid disobedience is just making things worse and worse?~~

~~You know what else you did that I told you not to do? You followed Dad to that bitch's house. The cat would have left a little trail, but you had to open it up wide by going there and make sure there was no chance of the Patron missing it. By the time you finish reading this, Dad will be dead and you know what? You killed him. We went through all this crap to make sure he wasn't home when the Patron came so you wouldn't see him murdered, but you couldn't leave well enough alone after that, could you? You might as well have put a gun to his head. Is that your solution for everything?~~

~~I'm sorry for that. I've never stopped being sorry for that. But you could have stopped it from ever happening in the first place.~~

Let me start over. We need to be calm about this.

When Melissa asked Olivia if she'd trade someone close's death for what she most desired, Olivia said yes. Melissa then asked her to do something—I'm not sure what—that led to the fire and the death of Olivia's sisters. Those deaths were needed as part of the ceremony to open the rent that let in the Patrons.

We didn't make any such agreement. We aren't responsible. I'm doing my best to show you how to make things better than they would be without our interference, but we aren't in charge of the world. Bad things—even horrible things—are going to happen whether or not we interfere, and there's nothing we can do about it.

When I was where you are I wanted to lash out and destroy the journal, make it a scapegoat for all the horrible things that have happened. That wouldn't change anything. If you somehow found a way to destroy it, then I'd never get it, and that would create a paradox the universe wouldn't let stand. We'd just move to a universe where I say the right thing and you don't destroy it.

We've reached the final turning point, the most important one. You need to be calm and detached. You need to relax and just let things go. There's nobody to tell you what to do. You could get drunk if you like. That might be fun to try. I can tell you from experience that if you drink enough the pain goes away and you just drift into sleep. You know where Dad's scotch is. If you prefer, you can try some of the pills from Mom's purse. She didn't take it when she left and they'll calm you right down. Doesn't that sound nice?

Do something to calm yourself. Then tell me how you feel and go to bed. We can talk more in the morning.

What the fuck are you talking about? You screamblame me and then cross it out and ignore it like it was never there? You don't think I'll notice that a Patron killed Dad because you drew a line through it? Am I an idiot to you that you think you can say "by the way, you probably just turned yourself into an orphan" under your breath and think I won't give it another thought? My dad is a fuckup but I LOVE HIM. How can you be like that telling me he's dead??

I am ending this. You and I killed Dad, killed strangers, probably killed Mom, got a baby's hands torn off, and unleashed a literal hell onto earth and your solution is for me to forget about it and fuck myself up with drugs and alcohol? Did it ever occur to you that there is a more permanent solution?

The Patrons make no sense. The journal makes no sense. It's all impossible. There is a point when things are bent so badly that you have to ask yourself whether it's more likely that all of reality has somehow been twisted into unrecognizability or that you've gone insane. Do you want me to believe that I'm the sane one when you quite literally have been telling me that I'm talking to myself? Isn't that a definition of insanity right there?

None of this would have happened if it weren't for you. Maybe bad things would have gone on anyway, but I wouldn't be responsible. Maybe I wouldn't have met

Eric, but I wouldn't have missed something that never happened. Maybe everyone would still be dead, but I wouldn't have a hand on the knife.

I can't stop bad things from happening, but I can stop you. If you never write this journal and you never make your devils' pact with Melissa, then I'm free, aren't I? And here's the beauty of it: if you're me, then to stop you, I just have to stop me.

It was your pointing out my blame that inspired me. You kept trying to talk me out of blaming myself, but you know as well as I do that I'm as full of guilt as you are of shit. When I saw there was no denying that, I went to Dad's office and got his .357 out of the cabinet. It feels cold against the side of my head. I'll bet you can't change the journal if I blow your head off, can you? That would fuck up your little plan, now, wouldn't it? If I kill you, you never write to me and NONE of this happens.

Let's see you bullshit your way out of that one. Say goodbye to your head, bitch. Enjoy the blood splatters!

DON'T SHOOT YOURSELF

USE THE RAZOR

CUT YOUR WRISTS

CUT YOUR WRISTS

God damn it. Is there no possible world where you don't shoot yourself? I added "no guns" to the initial list. I added the razor blades to the purchase list and made sure they were always handy.

When the journal is yours again, when you're in my position, you need to try harder. I think if you try too hard it raises suspicion too much, but if you don't try hard enough, this is inevitable. Maybe if you arranged things so you could easily take sleeping pills and alcohol that would be better. Or maybe you can find a way to get Dad to take the gun with him when he leaves.

Damn it! There has to be a way around this.

why am I alive

You can't die until this is done. Melissa saw to that. She can't have us completely derailing her plans.

The hole you shot in your stupid head is too big to heal so it's going to stay that way. You're going to be surprised by the size of the exit wound.

it hurts

Getting shot in the head does that. You don't hear about it because most people don't live long with so much of their brain and skull missing.

If I don't sound like I'm full of sympathy, it's because I'm not. I've had to live with this much longer than you have. The best I can do at this point is stop you from making any more mistakes so you can find a way to convince yourself to avoid this stupidity when it's your turn to write my portion of the journal.

The pain isn't going to stop. Mom has prescription pain meds that you can take, but don't take them now because you'll need them later. You can't write in the journal coherently without them.

Don't take aspirin; it just makes you bleed more. Extra strength Tylenol takes some of the edge off, and there's a little morphine in Dad's survival medical kit, but mostly you're just going to have to live with it. Pack the wounds with towels and cover them with Ace bandages (duct tape, when the bandages are too foul to use anymore).

When you can sleep, sleep sitting up. If you lie down, it bleeds too much even if it's packed. You won't bleed to death but it's disgusting and the loss of blood makes you delirious for a while.

Don't try to eat anything for at least half a day. The pain in your jaw is from slamming it into the desk when you fell. You lost a tooth. Don't look for it; it's not there.

i need help

Don't even think about it.

Even if you find a way to get to an ambulance or hospital, doctors will figure out pretty fast that there's something wrong with the girl who won't die and treat you like a threat because of everything going on. You'll be locked up forever. Maybe experimented on. And that's assuming nobody sees you walking around with a hole in your head and decides to raise a mob to cut off the zombie's head. For now, the outside world is just something you see through a window.

Forget about trying to explain anything to anyone. If you haven't noticed yet, you can't talk anymore. You apparently blew away something important in your speech center. All you can do is moan at this point, and that makes you look even more zombified. Your fine motor control is also just about shot and is only going to get worse, so writing is going to be out of the question in a day or two. You're going to want to lean on walls and furniture when you walk.

Stay in the house. Nobody is going to bother you there. The survival food from Costco is in the garage. You can't starve yourself to death, but starvation feels miserable. The power will be on for two more days, then off for three, then spotty after that. The internet and cable never come back. Dad's emergency radio works for a while, so use it to get news. Read books. Think about stories you want to write. Be patient.

After you read these instructions, put the binder clips back on the journal just like you found it. Leave it on the desk. In about three months a Patron is going to come with a package wrapped in purple construction paper and tied with twine. Trade the Patron the bag of prunes for its package. This package you can open, although experience has taught us that you'd open it anyway, hasn't it?

The package will be a letter from Melissa. That letter will have a list of things like the can of tuna that you need to remember to put in the journal. It will also have answers to all of your meaningful questions about the plane of separation, what is happening, and what will happen. Those answers will put your mind at ease about many things and will also highlight the importance of what we are doing.

With the letter will be a stylus Melissa made that lets you create type on paper by thinking words, but be careful because you can't erase. After you have that, open the journal again and you'll see that it only has your writing. The typing will be gone, and it will be your turn to send instructions.

I never did tell you why rule #6 was crossed out, did I? There used to be a rule that if I didn't answer when you wrote, you should just put the book away so that it could reach your future self who would write the response and send the book back in time. I think that's because the book had to travel up and down the time stream over and over to get filled up, but now that we've reached the end, it no longer matters. I've crossed out that rule and added a note to stop you from asking about it, which might mess up our conversation.

As you go through the journal, creating responses to your handwritten posts, you have to find a way to stop yourself from shooting yourself. Living with this pain is the most horrible thing you'll ever have to do, and trying to write coherently through it is close to impossible. If you don't shoot yourself you won't have this much pain and maybe there are things you can do differently or think of doing differently because your head is clearer. I don't know if it's impossible to stop you from becoming suicidal, but I think slit wrists would be easier for you to work around. I went for that this time, but the more I think about overdosing on sleeping pills the better I like that idea. You might recover from that completely. I suggest you give it a try. Don't forget!

If we follow Melissa's instructions and write in the journal so that her plans are completed she is going to heal me. Us. I'll get another package, this one with the vial that holds the tooth Melissa "removed." By putting that back in my mouth, my body will be restored to make me as healthy as the day we visited her. We're going to be okay and can look for Eric and Mom with a clear, pain-free head and without worrying about being captured or attacked, or of scaring them off once we've found them.

why didn't you warn me

I did everything I could. You'll see when you get here.

By the time you're in my position, you'll be desperate and hold on to any chance for hope you can find. I can't even describe what the world is like now. I don't want to look out the window because of what I might see, and I don't want to sit in the dark because of what I know will come to mind.

The uncertainty, the guilt, the pain, the desperation—I don't know which is worst. Maybe wondering about Eric. I only know he's alive because Melissa promised he is, but I have no way of knowing whether he's longing for me as strongly as I'm longing for him. I know we're in love, I believe that to the core of my heart, but with every day that passes I have to worry that he may have given up on me and moved on.

No matter what happens, you have to complete the journal. If you don't, there's no hope for us and no chance at all. We can't die until this is complete. If you do nothing, then you're going to end up living with the pain forever.

I hate you

I hate me, too. There's not a moment when I don't feel the regret I'm swimming in rising past my lips and sloshing into my mouth. Working this journal from the other end has forced me to live through my mistakes a second time in an endless avalanche of second-guessing, self-criticism, and desperate feelings of futility and impotence.

It's over now, though. We've done everything Melissa asked. She'll be here soon and we can start rebuilding. I am so close to being able to focus on the future instead of being pounded into hamburger by reminders of my shortcomings. No matter how bad the world is, I look forward to that.

tell me when

I will. As soon as I'm made right, I'll put an entry in the journal. Everything's going to be okay. Finally. You'll see.

Hello?

Made in the USA
Columbia, SC
25 May 2019